LAST STAND OF THE DEAD

WHITE FLAG OF THE DEAD BOOK VI

JOSEPH TALLUTO

CHAPTER 1

"Are you kidding me?" I was stunned stupid. There was no other way to describe it. I just couldn't believe what I was hearing. "They're right *there*! Just get a patrol across and find a way to pin them down!"

"Can't be done right now, sorry." Colonel Freeman seemed sincerely apologetic. "The damn truck is stuck and there's little we can do until the other truck gets in place."

"Unbelievable. They are right damn there, and your stupid soldier goes and blocks everything because he can't figure out what goddamn gear the goddamn truck is in! Jesus Christ!"

I was fit to be tied. We had finally managed to catch up to the little zombies that had been tearing across Iowa, and we finally had figured out how they were travelling undetected. But just as they slipped across the river into Illinois, some dumb ass manages to let them get away. I let the trooper know what I felt in no uncertain terms. Charlie was next to me and I could see he was as angry as I was.

"No offense, sir, but lighten the fuck up. It was a mistake. You've probably made the same, too," The soldier replied. He was shorter than I was, and although he had a layer of fat on him, there was still plenty of muscle underneath.

That was it. I didn't wind up, I just uppercut from the waist, taking the smart-ass on the chin and knocking him to the ground. In an instant, several of the troopers friends jumped in, and I had my hands full, blocking punches and dishing out punishment. The numbers actually worked for me, since there were too many of them to attack, all at once. I had my arm wrapped around one soldier's neck and was pulling on the ear of another, when a third stepped in front of me and pulled his fist back for a serious punch to my head. I couldn't do anything but watch it come when suddenly, the man's head snapped sideways and he fell to the ground.

1

Charlie had entered the fray. Between the two of us, we beat the crap out of the small platoon that had backed up the corporal who had caused the headaches in the first place. I took out my frustration by distributing busted noses, cracked ribs, and loose teeth.

When we dropped the last one, we turned back to the bridge and found ourselves staring at the muzzles of five rifles. Apparently, the men had friends who weren't happy with us.

"On the ground! *Now!*" One of the men shouted furiously.

Neither of us moved. I stared at the man in front of me who held the rifle with unsteady hands.

"Not likely. Put your weapons down. That's an order," I said.

"You don't give me orders. My orders come from Colonel Freeman. Get your ass on the ground or I will put you down." The soldier, whose name badge read Williams, took a small step forward to punctuate his words.

"Williams? Put that rifle down or I'll make you wish you had." I was calculating the odds, and I figured I could take the two on the left before they knew what was happening, and I knew Charlie was focusing on the two on the right. The one in the middle would be a problem, and I might have to take a bullet before I could get him. I didn't relish that idea, but I was just mad enough.

"That's enough!" Colonel Freeman's voice cut through the air. "Mr. Talon, Mr. James, would you please let us handle this?"

"Talon?" Williams said to himself, as he lowered his rifle. "No way."

I leaned in close as I went by. "Way." As I walked away towards our trucks, I overheard Colonel Freeman chewing out his men.

"Damn fools. You looking to get killed?" The colonel helped several of the men to their feet.

"I had the drop on him, sir," Williams said defensively.

"He'd have killed you for it, and if he didn't, his wife would have. And you're in serious shit for disobeying orders, soldier." Colonel Freeman pointed over to our trucks where Sarah was standing in the bed, a rifle at the ready to drop anyone foolish enough to start shooting.

"Whose orders, sir?" Williams was confused.

"*His*, jackass."

I lost the rest of the conversation as I reached the truck and helped Sarah down. We were about fifty yards on the bridge leading across the Mississippi from Iowa to Illinois. We had been chasing ghosts across the state for the better part of a week, and just as we thought we had the little zombies caught in a vise, they slipped across thanks to our oversight. With the delay caused by the truck, we were swiftly losing our tactical advantage and would have to start all over again chasing the little zombies.

When this all started, I had no idea what we were going up against. All we had known was several towns had fallen off the grid and three groups of investigators had disappeared. The mystery turned out to be a large group of zombie children, moving fast, infecting towns, and wiping out large portions of the post-upheaval communities. These zombies were fast, smart, and somehow able to communicate with each other. They were the deadliest things we had ever come across, and so far, had managed to outsmart all of us.

"You okay?" Sarah asked, taking my hand and looking over my knuckles. They were a little swollen, but not bloodied. Charlie at least had the presence of mind to have his gloves on, so his hands were fine.

"Our luck continues to hold," I said darkly, looking over at the soldiers who were getting to their feet and casting evil glares our way. I figured our welcome with this bunch was at an end, and I could honestly say, I was glad to be done with it.

"What are we going to do now?" asked Tommy. He and Duncan were at the van, both of them holding rifles and matching the soldiers glare for glare. Duncan was smiling and winking at the soldiers, and it was only a matter of time before some hothead tried to make a point.

I thought about it for a minute. "We're done. We found what the problem was; we got the army where they were supposed to be, so we just need to get the hell home and away from all of this. It's not our problem. We fulfilled our obligation."

Charlie spoke up. "Maybe so, but we can't just walk away and let this group of knuckleheads try and save the world. We'd be going back into a dead state."

Duncan and Tommy nodded, and I knew what they were saying was true.

"All right. All right. You're right, we can't just let it fly. If for no other reason than we need their firepower. I feel better for saying it though," I said.

That got a chuckle and we settled in to wait. I figured the truck would be cleared in a few minutes and we'd be on our way after the zombies within the next half hour.

It was a good plan, and I felt better for it.

CHAPTER 2

An hour and a half later, I was beyond fuming. I had left Madville a few miles down the road and was pulling up to Ragetown, with Insanityburg just over the hill. The soldiers had managed to fail in the removal of the stuck truck, but the other one, which was supposed to pull the stuck one out, had also become stuck in the roadbed. Apparently, the driver, a kid about seventeen, thought to take a shortcut around a car, and misread the embankment. Twelve soldiers were trying to push out a four-ton truck from a ditch and up a thirty-degree incline.

We weren't going anywhere from here. I was done, and the crew was too.

"Okay, we're leaving," I announced. Everyone agreed with me, and I went over to where the Colonel was berating his men for the delay.

"This is unacceptable! I can't believe we have the enemy within reach and we are stuck here on this goddamn bridge! Get men over to the other side right now! If nothing else, see if they can pick up some sign as to the enemy's direction, and we can get them later. You five, go!" Colonel Freeman was about as angry as I was, but I had to agree his suggestion made sense.

"Colonel Freeman?" I stepped up beside the man, ignoring the glares of the men with bruised and bloodied faces.

Freeman spun around, ready to unleash another tirade, but he saw it was me. His demeanor softened somewhat, but not by much.

"What can I do for you, Mr. Talon? We're trying as best we can." Freeman wiped his forehead with a small bandanna.

"We're going to take our trucks and head south, cross the river, and see if we can pick up the trail of the zombies. We'll move faster than the men you've placed over there, and we'll report to you their movements. Sound good?" I said.

Colonel Freeman thought about it as he watched his five men disappear over the bridge and head towards the railroad bridge that the little zombie kids had used.

"Sounds good. We're using channel three for routine communication, so you can reach us that way," he said.

"Thanks, I remember. We'll be seeing you." I shook his hand and went back to the truck and van, feeling a lot better that we were heading out and away from this mess. If they couldn't cross a bridge without trouble, I didn't want to be anywhere near them when the bullets started flying.

I told the crew what we were going to do and they all agreed. Duncan had a question, though.

"What the hell happened to the army?" He asked. "A few years ago, we kicked the crap out of the zombies, knocked them back to the mountains and sealed them away for good. This group would have been lunch in ten minutes."

Charlie fielded this one. "These aren't the same men who came with us to fight. The army we had was all veterans of the upheaval and had been surviving since day one. They had faced their zombie and killed it, before the war to take it all back began. When the call came to finish the job, every single one of them knew the enemy, knew what the Z's could do, and were ready for it. The ones who made mistakes were already dead. We could drop any of our group into zombie-infested areas and unless something went seriously wrong, they would be able to survive and get out, killing a hell of a lot of zombies along the way.

"These guys are the ones we left behind, because they weren't old enough to fight yet, and their fathers had been the ones to protect them from the zombies in the first place. They can shoot, but can they fight? Don't know for sure. The guys we fought with are scattered all over, taking their due from the peace they earned. We could get them back, but it would take weeks for the word to get out, and by the time we had enough together with the right supplies, the little zombies would have made their own army invincible."

I looked at Charlie in surprise, along with Tommy and Duncan. That was probably the longest speech I had ever heard Charlie make.

Shaking it off, I said, "Let's get going. Those zombies are getting further into Illinois with every minute, and we need to figure out where they're travelling."

We got back in the vehicles and slowly wound our way through the rest of the army, as they waited for the road to clear. Many of the men were lounging about, lying in the sun and just taking it easy. A couple was using the time to clean their rifles, and those were the ones I figured would do better than the others. They at least had their priorities straight, and could be certain of their guns' functionality in case of need.

We cleared the southern end of Burlington and made our way south. We had to detour several times, since the airport was in that area and was choked with cars that had never been removed. There was no place to put them, so they just stayed and rusted. I noticed none of them had any occupants, ghouls or otherwise, so this may have been one of those rare, orderly evacuations.

We took Madison Avenue out of the city proper and followed the river south. Sarah was looking nervous, but I didn't need to ask what was wrong. She was thinking about our children, and hoping to get there as quickly as possible. I didn't admit it out loud, but I was thinking the same thing. I had a bad feeling our screw-up at the bridge was going to cost us dearly.

Madison Avenue turned into County Road X62 for no apparent reason, and then it became Summer Street, since it turned a corner. We took Highway 61 south, which became 354th Ave just for the hell of it. Tommy called from the van and asked when we had returned to Ohio. I guess he had been paying attention to the street signs as well, as he was equally confused as to why the roads just couldn't be one name from beginning to end.

We passed by Hillcrest Memorial Park, a vast forested area with a little go-cart track on the east end. South of that, we reached the Great River Road and prepared to cross the bridge into Illinois. I stopped the truck and got out, with Sarah tossing me curious looks. I held up a finger to Charlie, who gave me a quizzical look as well.

The bridge was an interesting affair, combining a car bridge with a railroad bridge. The car part was on top as it crossed the river, and on the other side, the two separated and were next to each other before splitting completely. I hadn't seen one like it before and it caught my attention. The road rose sharply up and I couldn't see anything after twenty yards.

What also caught my attention was the three army trucks parked on the bridge, angled and arranged in such a way as to funnel attackers into a narrow choke point along the far north side, allowing for easier kills and greater control. Whoever had been in charge of this group knew what they were doing. That same person was currently missing, which had me curious as hell.

I pulled my rifle out of the back of the truck, and handed Sarah hers as well.

"What's the story?" Tommy asked, looking over the trucks on the bridge.

"Don't know yet," I said. "The trucks are here, they had to have gotten the message to rejoin the army by now. Where could they all have gone?"

Duncan moved cautiously over to the trucks and using the tip of his sword, eased the canvas back on the rear of the trucks. Sarah joined him and aiming her rifle as he opened the door, the two of them checked the cab of each vehicle.

Both of them returned quickly with more confusing news.

"No blood or any sign of trouble on any of the vehicles," Duncan said.

"The keys are even in the ignitions," added Sarah.

Stranger and stranger. "Okay, well, it really isn't our problem; they probably spent the night in some house and aren't back yet. Duncan and Tommy, get the two far vehicles backed up and out of the way, we'll be able to get around them. Charlie, you and Rebecca are with Sarah and I, we'll check the nearby houses and see if we can find them."

Heads nodded and we were about to move when Tommy shouted from the bridge.

"We've got company!"

CHAPTER 3

We all looked in Tommy's direction, and sure enough, there were five men moving slowly along the bridge. Even from this distance, we could tell who they were, and more importantly, what they were.

"Looks like they got caught out in the open," Charlie said, as he looked them over through his rifle scope.

"How bad?" I asked.

"Lot a bites, lot of blood," Charlie reported. "Looks like they died hard."

"No doubt," Sarah said, looking through her own scope. "Wonder if the rest are on the other side of the river."

"We'll see, I'm sure. Duncan! Watch yourself!" I yelled.

Duncan stood up on the running board of one of the trucks and looked towards the oncoming soldiers. He waved to us, and then took a minute to back the truck up. Parking it, he looked again at the oncoming zombies and I could see him calculating the timing. He must have figured he could get it done, so he ran to the next truck, and moved it back alongside the others. He got out just as the ghouls were stumbling into fighting range.

Duncan pulled out his pistol and fired three shots at the nearest ones, striking them in the head and knocking them to the ground.

I wish I could have seen Duncan's face when the Z's he had shot didn't stay down, they got back up and started moving for him again. But I did get to see his face as he raced back to our position. If ever there was a poster for "WTF," Duncan's face was it.

Charlie was the first to get the point across and clarify things for Duncan.

"Ever wonder why they're called 'bullet-proof helmets?'" He asked.

Duncan stared at Charlie for a moment. "Oh, geez." He wasn't as much embarrassed, as he was dreading the inevitable teasing that was going to follow once we finished up this business.

We all chuckled a bit, I watched as Sarah and Rebecca stabilized their rifles on the hood of the truck. Sarah fired first, sending a round through the eye of the closest zombie, dropping him to the ground.

Rebecca killed the next, shooting him dead before the first even hit the dust. Sarah followed suit and the next four were eliminated quickly.

I went over to the corpses to make sure they were dead, but it was clear they weren't coming back. The bullets had entered their heads, bounced off the Kevlar helmets, and reentered the skulls, seriously scrambling their signals. The clothing on several had been torn around the legs and arms, telling me there had been several attackers. A couple of the soldiers had huge tears in their throats, which told me that they had been attacked while they were sleepin, or had been finished off when they had been taken to the ground. Either way, it wasn't a good way to go.

Tommy joined me at the corpses, while the rest of the crew waited by the trucks.

"Something about this is sitting wrong, John," he said.

I looked around for any movement stirred up by the shots before answering. "Talk to me. What's on your mind?"

"If these guys had bunked in the trucks, they'd have been pretty safe from attack. So they had to be coaxed out." Tommy looked down at the soldiers. "How could they have been lured out?"

I shook my head. "We aren't going to find answers here, and the only place to get them is where they came from." I pointed to the other side of the river. "We have to get over there anyway."

We walked back to the trucks and I laid it out plain for the crew. "We're crossing here, and I don't know what's on the other side. Charlie and I will take point, Tommy and Duncan, you two ride in the truck bed and give us cover if we need it. Rebecca, you drive the van up front, we'll keep the side door open in case we need a retreat. Sarah, you're on the truck, make sure Duncan doesn't fall out."

"Hey!" Duncan protested. "One time! And it was a big bump you hit!"

We all laughed, and then got serious as we loaded and made ready. I had magazines within easy reach; my pickaxe and tomahawk were loosed and ready to go. My knife and pistol mags were within easy reach, and I figured if I was to cross over the great divide today, I was going to pay my way dearly.

Charlie and I walked ahead of the vehicles, but close enough for a quick retreat. Rebecca kept the van just slightly back and to the left of us, leaving an open door within easy reach. If it got bad, we could be inside within a second or two. I figured we still had five to ten soldiers to deal with, and possibly several zombie kids, so we had to be careful.

Charlie spoke up as we reached the top of the first hill, placing us directly above the railroad tracks that crossed the river.

"Figure the zombie kids did this?" He asked.

I nodded. "Can't be anyone else, except for new zombies made by the kids."

Charlie thought about that for a second. "You realize that this means the little Z's split their group up to make the crossing at two places."

"Yeah, I thought about that," I said. "We've got to tell Colonel Freeman as soon as we can, that his men down here are dead."

"Think the group to the north is dead, too?"

"No way of knowing yet, but if they are, we have some serious trouble on our hands." I said.

"How so?"

"This group probably won't come right at us, looking for a fight. We'll have to hunt them down and it's going to cost us a lot." I said.

"You worried, John?" Charlie asked, looking over at me.

"Hell, no," I said. "I'm scared shitless."

Charlie nodded. "Me, too."

CHAPTER 4

We stopped talking as we reached the middle of the river. The road narrowed a bit, and we could hear the gentle voice of the water below us as it moved around the pylons and artificial islands that held up the bridge. Apart from the threat of vicious attack by zombie children, and the fact that we could possibly be walking into as nasty an ambush as we had ever faced, the day was fairly pleasant.

"Movement," Charlie said, bringing up his rifle.

"How many?" I asked. My carbine didn't have a scope, so I was limited to my own eyes, and I didn't feel like pulling my binoculars out of my pack.

"Four, I can see, and it looks like there's another on the ground, moving, but not up," Charlie replied.

"Distance?" I flicked the safety off on my rifle and moved it to a more comfortable position.

"Three hundred, maybe three fifty." Charlie signaled to the truck and van that he had spotted movement, and I could see Duncan and Tommy settle in and find some kind of base on which to brace their rifles.

"I'll take the right side," I said, moving over to the side of the road. I had to be careful. These country bridges weren't built for pedestrians, and there was a lot of open space for a person to fall through. Come to think of it, there was a lot of space for a car to fall through. I shook my head and concentrated on the zombies that were shuffling around at the far end of the bridge.

There were four of them moving, and they were in their gear, which told me they had either been attacked last night before they had set up watches, or it had happened this morning, once they had gotten their day moving. I was hoping for this morning, so we could be only an hour or two behind the horde, but it probably wasn't going to happen.

We walked slowly over to the other side, and about halfway there, the zombies saw us and began to head in our direction. The one on the ground looked over to see where his friends went and started rolling our way as well. His legs were torn to pieces, which explained his vertical challenges.

When they were about fifty yards away, Charlie opened up on his side, shooting one in the face and the other in the knees. The second one had some problem where its head was rolling forward, so it was pretty well protected by the helmet.

I shot one on my side, then the other, not having the problem Charlie had. I went over to inspect my two, while Charlie finished off the second one, which was dragging itself across the pavement, and leaving dark streaks in its wake.

Mine had been bitten on the neck and arms, with additional bites on the face. The hands were torn up pretty bad as well. From where I sat, it looked like these guys had engaged the enemy and been overwhelmed. The big question was how come they left the safety of their trucks? By my reckoning, they could have taken a good chunk out of the enemy with little danger to themselves.

I stood up and walked over to where Charlie was finishing off the crawler. He didn't bother with his tomahawk, he just shot it at close range.

We kept walking and reached the edge of the bridge where it reached the other side of the river. There was a small grove of trees on the left of the road, and a mess of wild bushes on the right side, where the railroad tracks ran alongside. A bit further east, we could see the tracks and road split into north and south directions.

There were also several small zombie corpses lying about, and dozens of brass casings shining in the rising sun. Four cars had been parked in a rough diamond shape, and there were four zombie corpses draped over the hoods and roofs of two of the cars.

Charlie was looking around, and I left him alone while he read the signs. He was the best woodsman I had ever met, and his tracking skills made much more sense than my uninformed guessing.

After a minute, he straightened, and looked over at me. "Well, any idiot could figure out what happened here."

Sarah pulled up the truck and Tommy shouted down from the roof. "Looks like a fight here."

I grinned and ignored Tommy when he asked, "What?"

"Go ahead," I said.

Charlie wiped the smile off his face. "They set up this post as a fall back position from the trucks, but something distracted them at exactly the wrong moment. What it was, I couldn't tell you, nor could I tell you why the soldiers from the trucks would abandon their safety to come here. Just doesn't make sense."

"Maybe more than you think," I said cryptically, as I pointed eastward.

"What's that?" Charlie asked as he brought up his rifle with its scope.

"The only thing ever to get men to abandon their posts, since the dawn of warfare," I said.

CHAPTER 5

As we waited, a small car came rolling down the road. One of the tires was very low, but that didn't deter the driver from trying to get here as fast as humanly and mechanically possible.

The car hit a large bump, and there were several squeals from the passengers as the driver corrected badly, and nearly wound up in the ditch. I had my doubts as to the ability of the driver, and I moved into the relative safety of the four vehicles as the car came careening up and screeching to a halt. Charlie was collecting the weapons of the soldiers and checking for any spare ammunition. He kept a small bag around his shoulder for that purpose, and when he started doing it, he had to endure a lot of 'man-bag' ribbing, but the little bag had proved invaluable over the past few months.

The car stopped and the occupants spilled out, four girls and two guys, none of which was a day over nineteen. One of the men eyed Charlie and I with a more than a little belligerence, and I cocked an amused eyebrow at Charlie.

"My God, are they all dead?" One of the girls asked.

"How many were there?" I asked, hoping to have some survivors.

"Ten, my God, are they all dead?" She asked again.

"Yes, they're all dead. When did you leave them?" I asked.

The girl stopped looking at the dead soldiers and looked at me directly. She was a pretty, thin girl with long brunette hair that looked to be recently styled. My suspicions were becoming more confirmed as to what got the soldiers down this way. I matched her gaze and waited, trying to hold down my impatience. If the little zombies had hit recently, we might be able to catch them and deal some serious damage, or direct the army to the correct spot to set up an ambush.

"I'm sorry, but who are you? Did you kill them?" She said directly.

I noticed the other kids were milling about the car and the men were talking in low tones. I stuck a finger in the air and made a circular motion, and then answered the questions.

"Look miss, yes we killed them the second time. The first time it was done by zombies. See those bites and tears? Bullets don't do that. These guys were attacked and recently, by the amount of fresh blood that's around here," I said. "When did you last see them alive?"

The girl thought for a minute, and then looked back at her friends. One of the boys shook his head at her and she turned back to me. "I don't know," she said with a small shrug of her shoulders.

I was reminded then of a lot of the students I used to have that would answer in the same way. It was annoying then and it was annoying now. "Well, I would guess you've been gone an hour, and your leaving saved your lives. What we're tracking here is a group of zombie kids, fast and smart. If you wish to stay alive, and keep alive those you know, then you should get back in your car and get the hell home and tell your folks trouble is all around you."

The girl's eyes widened and she looked around into the brush and across the river. I didn't blame her, it was a natural reaction. She was old enough to remember the Upheaval, and in all likelihood, those memories weren't baby ducks and sunshine.

The girl nodded and ran back to the car, speaking quickly to her friends. The girls and one of the men looked around and quickly got into the car. The other man, the one who had shook his head at the girl, walked over with an angry look on his face.

"What about their weapons? If we're in danger, we should have their weapons," he said, stepping up to the small pile of corpses I had been making while speaking to the girl.

"You'll be fine. Go home, get your own weapons, and brace for an attack. If you're not attacked for three or four days, chances are, they've moved on." I said.

"Just give me one gun, then. You've got only six people and ten more guns than you need. You can't just leave us defenseless." The man said this with a sly smile, which I am sure he thought was charming. I wondered if he actually practiced it.

I thought about it, and then relented. I took one of the rifles and made sure it was unloaded. I handed it to the boy and watched as he looked it over. Charlie threw a quizzical look my way as I did that.

"What about ammo?" The kid asked, holding the weapon down and away from everyone.

"Not yet," I said. I took the magazine for the rifle and walked over to the car. I handed it to the other man and spoke to him for a few seconds. The first boy came back to the car and put the rifle alongside the seat, next to him in the front.

As I walked away, the car backed up, and slowly drove out of sight, turning off a side road and heading in a southerly direction.

Charlie approached me. "How come you gave them a gun and ammo? Weren't you worried he might try to take a shot at you?"

I shrugged. "That's why I took the mag out. I told the other guy not to give it to his friend until they were out of sight. I also told them they were facing at least fifty zombies, which was twenty more than they had bullets for. I figured they'd save their ammo."

"So they were the ones that got the soldiers down here, huh?" Charlie asked, changing the subject.

"Yeah, one or two of the girls must have run across the soldiers, and said they'd be back with friends. In the meantime, the other soldiers back at the trucks heard about the party and wanted to join in. Trouble is, the party wasn't what they had hoped for," I said.

"Sounds about right. How'd they get jumped so badly?"

I pointed to the bridge. "The little Zs came across on the railroad part, so they were hidden until the tracks and the bridge separated, which is only about thirty yards back. Hell, regular zombies could have jumped this crew, let alone fast ones."

"All right. Next move?" Charlie said, walking over to the van. Tommy and Duncan jumped out of the bed of the truck, Duncan electing to ride with Sarah and myself for a bit.

"Let's get rolling and see what towns are on this heading. We need to make up some time and get this horde nailed down," I said.

"All right, we're behind you," Charlie said, as he closed the van door and secured his rifle.

I climbed into the truck and Sarah smiled at me. "Cheer up, we're almost home."

I smiled back, but inside I was worried. We were close to home, closer than we'd been in days.

But so were the zombies.

CHAPTER 6

"Come out, come out, wherever you are, you little bastard," Duncan said, slowly walking through the aisles of a small grocery store. I could hear him talking to himself the next aisle over, and I could also hear Sarah laugh a little in response, while she walked down the aisle on the other side.

"Watch for the friends, these things never attack alone." I said quietly to both of them.

"Clear on my side," Sarah said.

"So far so good, although it looks like the chili has expired," Duncan said.

"Dare you to eat it," I said.

"I prefer to keep my guts inside, thank you."

"Double dare you!" Sarah called from the other aisle.

"You first," Duncan said.

We had crossed the bridge into Illinois a half hour ago, and made our way east as best we could. We knew the little zombies were around us somewhere, but didn't have a notion as to where. We were chasing a small group, detached from the main horde, and I was hoping to have them lead us to them. But as we worked our way through a small town, Tommy had spotted a small group of them out in the open. We chased them to this small grocery store and the three of us chose to go in. Charlie, Rebecca, and Tommy were outside, making sure none of the kids got away.

Ordinarily we would have been quieter, but I wanted to draw them out, make enough noise to drive them crazy and attack us. We were in good spots. They couldn't attack any more than two across, and Tommy had reported only seeing five of them. So we were in here trying to get them out and kill them.

"Quiet!" I hissed. "Listen."

Sarah and Duncan silenced immediately, and we all stood stock-still. A few seconds later, we could hear it.

Click click click click. Click click click click.

We had all heard that sound before, and we all knew what it was. They were in here, and they were getting ready to attack.

That clicking seemed to be one way they communicated with each other.

"Get up on the shelves, quietly," I whispered.

I moved as silently as I could, which wasn't too hard, since the shelves were empty. This town had been a casualty of the zombie wars, and everything of use and everything resembling food was taken away for the effort. On the top shelf, I saw Duncan and Sarah had already beaten me to the top. There was only about three feet of space between the shelf and the ceiling, so it was going to be tight, but we didn't have a lot of choice.

I signaled to Duncan to make some noise, and he responded by throwing a small piece of wood he had found. Sarah readied her weapon, and I readied mine.

Duncan threw the block down the aisle, and when it reached the end, a little zombie jumped out at it. Sarah popped it in the head and dropped it.

That seemed to be some kind of signal. Five little zombies suddenly tore around the corners of the aisles, running full tilt down the centers, their eyes wide and their mouths twisted in vicious leers. There were three boys and two girls, each of them had a pale color of clay. None of them looked to have been a day over eight years of age when they died.

Two were in Duncan's aisle and two were in Sarah's. I had a little girl in mine, and they all stopped about halfway down the aisles in what could only be described as bewilderment, if that was possible in a zombie.

Five shots later, Duncan and Sarah climbed down off their shelves. I was halfway down when a small snarl got my attention. I looked at the end of my aisle and a small boy was racing towards me. I dropped to the ground, tripping on the girl I had shot, and fell against the shelves. My rifle was pinned to the shelf by my weight, and I was off balance with my right arm pinned to the shelf.

The little Z threw himself at me, and I used my left arm to push myself off the shelf. My foot caught on the girl on the floor and I fell over the prostrate form of the other ghoul, dropping my rifle in the process, while the moving zombie crashed into the space I had just vacated. I got up on one knee, just as the boy spun to the attack, and I grabbed for my 'hawk as he threw himself at me again, arms outstretched.

The blade end of the trench hawk slammed into the collarbone of the Z, embedding itself and taking the kid to the floor. He grabbed at my legs, and managed to get a grip on my pants, pulling himself closer for a bite.

No thanks. I pushed back on the hawk with my left hand, burying it deeper into his neck and keeping his face away from my flesh, and pulled my pistol with my right. A single, very loud .45 report ended the career of the little zombie in a nameless town in a minor grocery store.

Sarah and Duncan appeared just as suddenly as the zombie, with their weapons up and pointing at me, uncomfortably.

"You good?" Duncan asked.

"Yeah, fine, just be careful, there may be more." I looked at Sarah. "I need to talk to Tommy about his ability to count."

Sarah smiled. "Go easy on him. He was counting from two hundred yards away."

"True." I looked around. "Well, at least we can say we won this one."

Sarah put an arm around me as we walked out the door. "Finally. Maybe this is the turning point."

"God, I hope so."

We moved outside and saw the relieved faces of our friends. I didn't have to give Tommy a hard time, Duncan took care of that for me. Charlie and Rebecca came over to Sarah and I, and we discussed further plans.

"Tried to get hold of Colonel Freeman, but the operator on their end said he was busy, but would relay a message," Charlie said.

"Did you tell him about the troops?" I asked.

"Nope. I just told him he wouldn't be seeing his southern platoon anymore, and Colonel Freeman could call us back for details."

I laughed. "That will get his attention. Good job. I'm sure he'll send men for the trucks, at least."

"If he doesn't, I say we snare one or two later for our own use," Charlie said.

"We'll worry about that later. Right now, we need to clear this area. I have a feeling we're going to be hunting little zombies for a while," I said.

"Let's do it."

The town was small, so it took us just a little time to clear it out. Charlie walked in a wide circle around the entire town, looking for any sign that the little zombies had passed that way. If there were, we'd have a general direction in which to follow and possibly a trail.

The rest of us poked around the town, checking any open doors or dark places. We didn't have any evidence that the little zombies were smart enough to close doors after themselves, and we hadn't seen them do much besides wait in ambush, so this cleanup was relatively easy.

When we finished the town, we waited for Charlie to return. Sarah and I chatted about our kids and how different they were. Aaron was getting to be a big boy, and I figured he probably be bigger than Jake some day. Sarah disagreed, she thought Jake would be the bigger one, but time would have to tell.

Tommy and Duncan compared daddy notes on their little ones, and fortunately for all of us, Charlie returned just as the debate over poop smell was getting under way.

"What news, Dan'l Boone?" Duncan asked.

Charlie gave that only a single eye roll and went to the back of the truck. He pulled out a map and laid it on the truck bed.

"I found tracks to the north, but not many. I'd say the six you finished in the grocery store were about a third of what came through here. I found tracks leading off in that direction." Charlie pointed northeast, "and I figure they are probably making their way along the railroad, like they were in Iowa."

"What's the next town along the tracks?" I asked, looking over.

"Map says Lomax, which is directly south of the crossing at Burlington."

"Think they're trying to regroup?" Rebecca asked.

"That'd be a level of sophistication I'd be scared to contemplate," Tommy replied.

We all nodded. We had to alter our attack plans to deal with a smarter group of zombies, what had killed other groups was their not adapting fast enough. I hoped our army, such as it was, would be able to deal with the new threat.

CHAPTER 7

We headed north along 130, taking care to try and pick up the trail of the zombies. Charlie was in the bed of the pickup with the biggest pair of binoculars we could give him. At each road crossing, we would slow down and he would scan for movement. Lomax was just a few miles along the road, and I was hoping we'd get there before another massacre occurred.

Tommy radioed from the van, and told us he had contact with Colonel Freeman. Freeman was angry his men had been killed, but there was nothing to be done for it now. He had asked us to be his southern flank, but Tommy had refused. I agreed with that decision. I did not want to be obligated to the army in case we had to get the hell out of Dodge and take care of our own. I asked Tommy if there was anything more to the message, and Tommy said we'd likely see the army again pretty soon.

"Why?" I had to ask. The army should have been racing to set up perimeters and ambush zombies.

"Freeman is sending the army out in small groups, hoping to cross the trail of the zombies and get a read on where they are going."

Jesus Christ. The one damn thing guaranteed to fail. I spoke out loudly.

"Dammit. Get him back on the radio. I need to talk to him." I pulled the truck over and waited for the van to pull up. I got inside just as the Colonel's voice came over the speakers.

"What do you need, Mr. Talon?" Freeman asked politely.

"Colonel, are you planning on sending out all of your men on limited reconnaissance?" I asked point-blank.

"Yes, Mr. Talon. I think it a good measure to send all the men out on a hunt and kill mission. We'll whip these little bastards at their own game," Colonel Freeman said.

"Colonel Freeman, with all due respect, you're going to get these men killed. You haven't faced them four times and we have. We know now what we are dealing with, and breaking the men into small groups will kill them." I nearly added, 'You damn fool', but figured it wouldn't advance my case very much.

"I'll think about it. In the meantime, we'll be deploying along the north and south of Route 34, so be alert for my men," Colonel said as a way of finishing the conversation.

"I'll be alert for their corpses," I said darkly, as I switched the radio off. I knew it was hopeless, but I could hold out for a small chance that the soldiers might actually be up to par and get the job done.

I turned to the assembled crew. "We should get moving, and try to find out where they are. The best thing we can do for the situation is to just report movement as we see it."

"We going to engage?" Duncan asked.

"Only if we can win," I said. "I'm not going to risk my neck out here when my home might be under attack in the future."

Any further discussion was cut off by Charlie yelling at us from the top of the truck. "I got movement! Town limits of Lomax. Looks like they've been hit!"

"Here we go again," I said as I ran to the pickup.

"You'd rather be fishing?" Sarah asked as she grabbed her rifle from the bed of the truck.

"Not really," I said. While I didn't enjoy hunting zombies, I really didn't enjoy fishing. Couldn't explain why to anyone. I just didn't have the patience for it. Maybe there wasn't any thrill like there was with chasing down Z's. Although the fish didn't try to eat you, it just wasn't the same.

CHAPTER 8

Lomax was located just a few miles away from the river, and they had the railroad running along side it, so with the little zombies, it wasn't a matter of if they were going to get hit, it was just a matter of when.

We raced up Route 130 and passed the sign that told us it was becoming 175N. I could see the railroad right next to the road and couldn't help but think, we could have saved ourselves a lot of trouble if we had just gotten here sooner. Damn delays cost us some lives.

At the edge of Lomax, we pulled up and took a serious look around. The town was very small, and by the looks of things, it had been largely abandoned a while ago. Only a few houses looked like they had any residents in them, and they were the only ones left around.

Charlie and I took point, and Sarah and Rebecca followed at a small distance, well separated to provide us cover with their higher-powered rifles. Duncan and Tommy followed at a larger distance, covering our backs. We developed this system during the zombie wars, when the Z's had taken to the buildings. Often they would see the two groups move past, then make their way out to try and hit from behind, only to get taken down by the two that hadn't shown up yet. The people bringing up the rear tended to get the most action, so we rotated a lot just to keep from getting burned out. Duncan liked it, though, and volunteered more than his share. I didn't mind, I liked point better, anyway.

Route 96, or 175N, or 130N, took us through the center of town, so we stuck to that path. A couple of the zombies that Charlie had seen were out in the fields, but they started a fast walk towards us when we came into view. One was a man in his late thirties, and the other was a woman about the same age. I figured they were probably married, and died together. I was curious if they had had any children, and if they might have survived.

I was watching the zombie movement, figuring out angles of attack, when Sarah called out my name. I looked back and she was pointing to a row of five houses. All of them were along the main road, but that wasn't what got my attention. All of them looked like they had been lived in and all of them had children's toys in the yards. Not a good sign.

"Sarah, you and Rebecca check out the houses, Tommy and Duncan, back them up. We'll take care of these two," I said. Charlie slung his rifle over his shoulder and took out one of his 'hawks. I followed suit, but I pulled out my pickaxe instead.

Sarah and Rebecca walked quickly to the houses and with Duncan and Tommy checking windows, they ducked inside.

Charlie and I walked over to the couple headed our way. The husband looked normal enough, save for the bloodied shirt and torn neck he was sporting. The woman, for whatever reason, just seemed to irritate me. She was a short, heavier zombie, with long black hair that probably was as lank in the living world as it looked in the dead one. Her face was long, but pinched, and she had small piggy eyes that stared out of her fat face. I don't know why she annoyed me, maybe she reminded me of someone I had dealings with in a former life, but I was going to take a small measure of joy in killing this creature.

She took small, waddling steps towards me, stumbling slightly over a few errant rocks in the grass. Her face and arms were torn, but her throat hadn't been opened like her husband. She raised a fat arm at me, and I waited for her to try and cross a small ditch before taking her out.

Charlie jumped the ditch and took out the man, a small, balding specimen with lots of blue tattoos on his arms. Charlie just pushed him over and killed him as he crawled to get up.

Mine stumbled face first into the ditch, landing heavily on the other side. Her arms flew out and she was face-planted in the tall grass. Her knees were at the bottom, and her feet were up the other side. It would have been difficult for her to get up out of there. I took the opportunity to crack her skull with the pointed end of my pick, and left her there in the ditch.

Charlie came back and looked at the dead woman. "That looks like it was nasty when it was alive."

I nodded. "I was thinking the same thing. For some reason…"

My reply was cut off, as a burst of firing erupted from the third house down the row that Sarah and Rebecca were going to check.

Charlie and I didn't even hesitate, we just ran towards the houses. We didn't run directly to the trouble, since the rest of the crew wasn't expecting us and would fire in our direction, not knowing we were there. We ran close to the first house, and then made our way across the yards when there was another crash of gunfire. We moved as quickly as we could, but the overgrown side yards had hidden vines and grasses that tugged at our feet.

"Sarah! Rebecca! We're on the south end! You all right?" I yelled as we approached the third house from the side.

"Be right there!" Sarah called. Her voice didn't seem to be concerned with anything, so I figured the situation was under control.

We waited for a minute, and then the four of them came strolling out the front door. Duncan was grinning like a loon, while Tommy was scowling. The two women were stifling giggles, so I knew this was going to be a doozey.

"How'd it go?" I asked.

Sarah spoke up. "The first two houses had two and four adults in them, respectively. They weren't any trouble at all. The third had a couple and some teenagers, maybe orphans they picked up from the area. Anyway, that's it for us. Duncan?"

Duncan laughed and picked up the narrative. "Tommy was upstairs in the house and heard something in a closet, so he opens it up and lets out four seriously pissed off cats."

Tommy, to his credit, said nothing at this point.

Duncan continued. "Tommy falls back, thinking they're little zombies and opens up, wounding three and killing one. So then we had to hunt down these cats and finish them off."

Tommy didn't say a word. He really didn't have to. Duncan had screwed up so many times that it would take a computer to chronicle them all.

Duncan turned to Tommy. "I'm not laughing at your mistake, dude. Just the look on your face when those furry things came leaping out at you."

Tommy reached up and thumped Duncan on the head, forgiving him for laughing and signaling we should get back to work. I agreed.

I turned to Sarah. "Any little kids?"

Sarah sadly shook her head. "Not here."

I nodded. It was what I expected. "Tommy, find somewhere high and check around for any movement. We need to keep moving."

Charlie and I resumed our walk through the town, with Rebecca and Sarah covering us. I didn't expect to find any more zombies, they would have come out at the sound of the shots.

As I looked into a pink building creatively named, 'The Pink', Charlie tossed a question to me.

"You ever wonder what happened to Zeus?"

That took me back. I hadn't thought about that cat in years. We'd picked him up on our trip to DC, and lost him when we crashed into the Smithsonian. I figured he probably never made it out of DC, and said the same to Charlie.

" I'm just guessing," I said, "For all I know, the little guy escaped and is living in some forest between here and there. Why?"

Charlie scanned the porch of a small motel before replying, "Just thinking about cats."

I looked back at Sarah who just shrugged. I knew how hard it was to catch a cat, but even the slickest of those little suckers couldn't evade the grasp of thousands of zombies forever. Chances were, little Zeus, or big Zeus now, was long gone.

CHAPTER 9

We reached the end of the town, and for some reason, I was more depressed than when we started. The town was small, but for the life of me, I couldn't really come up with a reason it existed in the first place. It didn't touch the river, the railroad was too far north, there wasn't any industry, and the houses didn't follow any pattern I could see. I couldn't imagine growing up in this place and not being bored out of my skull on a weekly basis.

Our search concluded, we walked quickly back to the trucks. I noticed as we were mounting up that two crows were picking at the body of the woman I had killed. "Good riddance," I said softly.

"What?" Sarah asked, buckling in.

"Nothing," I said. "Nothing at all."

We headed north, and I was hoping we would run into some of Freeman's men, but as we followed Carmann Road, I wasn't seeing anything, or hearing anything on the radio. Tommy had reported that he had seen some mowed down grass to the north, but we would have to take a backcountry road to get there.

I didn't have any other plan, so when we hit 575N, which incidentally went east and west, I took the road east.

We travelled about a half mile before we spotted them. They were walking along the road in single file, being led by a boy about six to nine years old. The ones in the back were smaller, but they were not as ragged or bloody as the first three. My guess would be the ones in the rear were the new recruits, being led by the older ones.

I slowed the truck down to a crawl, keeping it moving the same speed as the zombies. They were walking briskly, but seemed only interested in following the road. We were about three hundred yards behind them and there was a decent breeze, which made enough noise in the long vegetation to cover our approach.

I stopped the truck just behind a small curve in the road, which would keep us from being seen. The road went through a small copse of trees, for about a quarter mile, from the look of it.

I got out of the truck and grabbed my rifle, Sarah right behind me. I jogged over to the van and met everyone as they came outside.

"We have one shot at nailing them before they scatter into the weeds, and it would be a nightmare to chase them down. So here's what we're going to do."

I outlined the plan carefully, and the only one to complain was Sarah, but she was only complaining because I was the one taking the biggest risk.

We moved carefully but swiftly, trying to get into position before we were spotted. If they saw us or smelled us, we'd have trouble, and I was actually more worried about delay than anything else. If we could get this group nailed down, I'd say we'd be safe in saying we'd secured the portion of the horde that had made the southern crossing of the Mississippi.

As we reached the woods, Rebecca and Sarah split off on the left and right sides of the road, blending into the trees and finding suitable firing positions. Further in, Tommy and Duncan ghosted off into the woods. About two hundred yards later, Charlie disappeared without a sound. The woods ended in another hundred yards, and I could see the little zombies trudging along. This was the big catch of the plan. In order for this to work, the zombies had to chase me right through the woods. I had to hope my aging legs could get me moving fast enough.

I jogged a little ways forward, closing the gap, and then yelled out, "Hey! You kids okay?"

You would have thought I had electrified the road. The group jumped around and stared at me for a minute, and then the older ones raced towards me, their dark eyes locking on me and their lips baring their teeth. The younger ones followed suit, racing after the older ones as best they could.

I waited for two heartbeats, and then spun around and ran. They were right on my tail, and as I pelted down the road, I wondered if I hadn't cut it too close. Halfway through the woods, I snuck a glance to the left and right and saw my crew readying their guns. They were going to wait until Charlie made his move, which I hoped was very soon.

The air was split by the sound of a high-powered round cracking through the air, and passing uncomfortably close to my ear. Several snarls and high-pitched wheezes flew through the wind as the zombies spun around to the new threat from their rear. They advanced only a few feet, before the reports of four rifles brought them down. The leader, a bigger boy, turned around again and ran for me, only to be put down by my wife's unerring aim.

"Thanks, honey!" I called, lowering my rifle.

"You're welcome!"

I waited for the crew to come out from their trees. We dragged the bodies off into the ditches, and as usual, I felt a small pang at the loss of life of the younger ones. Sarah picked up on it right away.

"It doesn't get any easier, does it?" She asked, putting a hand on my arm.

I looked down at her. "No. These guys never had a chance." I looked over at Charlie.

"You shot was a little close, my friend," I chided.

Charlie looked sheepish. "You went to the right just as I shot. Scared the shit out of me, thanks very much."

"Scared the shit out of *you*?" I asked. "I could have turned my head and kissed that bullet."

Charlie shook his head. "Quit running like a girl and we won't have any problems. OW!"

I didn't have to answer that, because Rebecca took up the charge and kicked Charlie in the shin.

"Let's get moving, if we're lucky, we can hook up with Freeman and get a better plan hammered into his head," I said, moving back to the trucks.

"What if he doesn't want to listen?" Tommy asked.

"Then we probably will have to make a call to the president and have him relieved of command," I said. "Do I want to do that? No, but if I have no choice but to watch men and towns die, I'll have to get it done." I looked into the face of each of my crewmembers and said, "Believe me, all I want to do is get this done and get home, just like the rest of you."

We left it at that and headed along the road. The going was rough, and there were a lot of washouts that needed to be traversed with care, especially around the crossroads. One was nearly a foot wide, and we lost a good twenty minutes while Charlie and I attacked it with small spades and filled in the ditch so we could cross.

Back on track, we worked our way north, trying to see if there was any sign of the army. There were no towns in this region, just isolated farms and homes, most of which were empty. The ones we did find occupied were warned about the danger and told to fort up, especially at night. Everyone we met was a veteran of the Upheaval or the Zombie Wars, so they knew what to do, and with the new threat explained, would unlikely be overwhelmed. These were the people that had made up our original army, and they would not go quietly into that dark night.

We were about fifteen miles from where we thought the army would be when we saw the smoke. It wasn't a lot of smoke, but it was oily black and thick. No one with any sense on the frontier would make a fire like that, so my first thought was that it was trouble.

"Do we check it out?" Sarah asked.

"Have to," I said. "If it's an idiot burning garbage, he just raised a flag to our little friends to come and get him. If it's an attack, we at least have another trail to follow and hopefully, we can ambush another set of the monsters."

Charlie radioed from the van. "You see the smoke?"

"On it. Hang back and get Rebecca ready to cover from the top."

"Done."

Charlie would pull back with the van, and Rebecca would poke the top half of herself through the roof hatch with her rifle. She'd see a little further than we would, and could nail anything coming at us that didn't wait for the van.

As ready as we could ever be, we headed for the source of the smoke that rolled lazily into the noon sky.

CHAPTER 10

"Jesus."

"How many down?"

"Can't tell from here, but it's bad."

"Are they up yet?"

"Not all of them, a few by the burning truck."

"Jesus."

"Yeah."

"We'd better get down there and start finishing them off."

"Yeah."

We followed the line of smoke up from the south, not really sure what we'd find. I was hoping it was just some damn fool burning his garbage, like we all did, and it got away from him. I did not expect to find what was waiting for us.

When we were near enough to the source of the smoke, we pulled over and crept up to the top of a small hill. There, hidden by a couple of bushes and tall grasses, we were able to see what was going on.

The scene wasn't pretty. The smoke was caused by a burning army truck, overturned in a ditch. Several men were laying about the truck, casualties of the accident. A second truck was stopped by the first one, and more bodies were scattered about. These were bloody and torn, and it didn't take much to figure out what had happened. Something had gotten in front of the first truck, causing it to swerve. The second truck had stopped to help with the accident, and had been ambushed. At this point, it was impossible to tell whether the first accident was caused deliberately, or had simply been bad luck. Either way, another twenty to thirty soldiers were down. Freeman was going to be pissed.

"Charlie, see if you can pick up a trail, or anything else." I looked at Charlie and he understood exactly what I was asking. "Tommy, you go with him. We're going to go and clean up as best we can."

We drove slowly down to the trucks, and parked on the southern end. Two of the soldiers rose from the ground to greet us, and Duncan popped them both. I circled wide, not wanting to be too close to the trucks and get nabbed from underneath. I worked my pickaxe on the ones that were still inert, and Rebecca and Sarah did the same. It wasn't easy, since half of them were still wearing helmets, so we had to cut their helmets off first, and then crack their skulls. Duncan just stabbed his big sword through their face, and that seemed to work just fine.

Another soldier rose to greet me, and this one was a big boy. He had to be six foot four and was thick in the shoulders and arms. If he grabbed me, he still had enough strength in there to pull me in tight for a hello chomp. I used my pick to hook his knee, and nearly wrenched my own arm out of its socket pulling that dude down. He landed hard on his back, with his helmet bouncing off the asphalt. I jumped on top of him, kneeling on his chest and using my free leg to pin down his arm. The other one reached for me, but I shoved my knife up under his chin and had just enough force to penetrate his brain. With a deep sigh, the young soldier died and slumped down.

We used the flames to purge our weapons, and then Rebecca grabbed a fire extinguisher from the still-functional truck, and sprayed out the fire from the overturned one, ending the signal to the rest of the world that something of interest was here. It also took the can from the overturned truck to do it, but it got done. We waited quietly for a moment and Duncan asked me a question.

"Should we take the truck with us?"

I thought for a moment, and then looked over at Sarah. She just shrugged her shoulders at me, and that was it. "Why not? You feel like driving it?"

Duncan nodded. He climbed aboard the truck, and then immediately jumped out.

"Something's in the back and it's moving!"

We all whipped our weapons up, and I moved slowly around to the back of the vehicle. Sarah and Rebecca covered the back of the truck as I pulled the canvas back and out of the way. I watched the two of them, and they didn't fire, but they didn't lower their weapons, either. I walked wide and joined them out away from the truck.

"Okay, I'm open to suggestions," I said.

"Can we keep it?" Duncan asked.

"I think we should just let it go," Rebecca said.

"What if it doesn't want to leave the truck?" Sarah asked.

"I think we can manage something," I said.

We all looked at the biggest damn German Shepherd I had ever seen. This pup must have weighed one twenty five, if he weighed a pound, and he was staring back at us with an intensity usually reserved for something about to be eaten. I didn't want to shoot the dog, it hadn't done anything, but bringing it with us was out of the question.

I released the latch that held up the rear gate and the dog jumped out, sniffing us and getting a general nose of the area. He looked at us for a moment, and then scampered off into the tall grass.

"That's too bad. I was hoping we could take it with us," Duncan said as he watched the grass for a moment, likely hoping it would come back.

"Wouldn't have worked, and you of all people know it," Tommy said.

"That's true, but it looked like a nice animal," Duncan replied.

We took a moment to drag the corpses off the road and decide our next move. Sarah took me to the side and asked about the dog. "Why couldn't we have taken it?" She wanted to know.

"We didn't train it," I explained. "We don't know what the command words are, and it would take too long to try and figure out. You want to be the one who says the wrong thing and suddenly that pile of fur and fangs is attacking Jake or Aaron? Not a chance."

Sarah looked thoughtful. "Didn't think about that. Do you think he'll be okay out there by himself?"

I chuckled. "Better him than whatever meets him when he's hungry."

CHAPTER 11

We drove north again, and managed to connect with Route 34 once more. It seemed to me that our destiny with that road wasn't over, and I turned east to start the search for the army and to get closer to home.

Duncan radioed over from the truck; he had better luck getting in touch with Freeman. He reported that Freeman took the news of the loss of his men hard, and was glad we had cleaned up as best we could. He told us he was setting up a line of defense around Kirkwood, and the line would extend from 164 to 116. It would be thin, but he thought they could delay them enough for reinforcements wherever the zombies attacked. They had reports of activity in the area, so they were confident that they were about to engage the enemy.

I thought about it as Sarah pulled out a map and checked the numbers. Kirkwood was as big a town as we could expect in these parts, and I had no idea if it was alive or dead. There were two towns on the way to Kirkwood, and we were going to have to visit both.

I called Duncan back and told him to relay our position to the Colonel, and we would be seeing him at Kirkwood shortly.

"What do you think, John?" Sarah asked.

"I think it's the best plan we have right now, provided Freeman got ahead of the zombies. If he's setting up after they left, he's going to look like a damn fool," I said.

"Where do you think the little zombies are right now?" she asked, looking over the map.

"They have to be close. That group that killed the soldiers we just left was heading north, but they could have turned. With luck, they're cross country right now and are slowing down enough for us to catch them." I pointed at the map. "Right now, I'd say they are about in this area." I circled a section north of Stronghurst.

"Let's hope you're right. I'm getting tired of this chase," Sarah said, putting away the map.

I looked over at her, and saw her hair falling forward on her face as she concentrated on folding the map. She didn't see me looking, and I got my eyes back on the road quickly enough, but it was just enough time to put another mental picture in my head to fall in love all over again with this woman. I didn't know what I'd do if I lost her. I really didn't.

My reflections were broken by Tommy calling over the radio. "Gladstone's been hit! They just got hit!"

The map came out again. We were five miles away. I radioed back. "We're there. Call the Colonel and let him know. This may be the one we've been looking for."

"Roger that, out."

I looked over at Sarah. "Full gear this time. Take no chances."

"Got it. You, too."

"Definitely."

We raced around a large bend on 34, and drove as fast as we could towards Gladstone. It was a little bit off the beaten path of 34, but as Sarah pointed out, it was right in line with the railroad tracks that had crossed the river at Burlington. Gladstone had survived the Upheaval due to geography. It was in the middle of nowhere and anywhere, and slightly south of never heard of it.

We reached the southern end of Gladstone about ten minutes after Tommy had alerted us. As we came up around a bend, I could see what might have been a problem for a town now that wasn't a problem for the Upheaval. This was a train town, and the tracks led along the northern border of the town. It wasn't hard to figure out how the zombies had attacked.

As we turned up Walnut Street, the town was in chaos. Two buildings were on fire, and there were several people lying around. One person turned to us as we drove slowly past, but he didn't see us. He was focused on his wife who lay in a pool of blood at his feet. He was holding a length of pipe in his hand and we knew exactly what he was waiting for.

Further in, we passed the fire district building, and I pulled over as a man stepped out and flagged us down.

"You're too late! They hit us about thirty minutes ago, pulled out about ten minutes ago." The man looked haggard, like he wasn't used to making serious decisions on a minute to minute basis.

I looked at the building. It was being used as a treatment center, but it was easy to see they weren't treating anyone who was going to live. There were about fifteen people lying on the ground, most of them holding small wounds and looking sick. I knew in about twenty minutes that this town was going to have another visit from the dead.

"What happened?" I asked, looking around. Several more people had seen us pull up, and were coming over to see what was going on. I cast a look over at Charlie, and he relayed the news to the rest of the crew. In situations like this, emotions ran high, and people said and did things they would later regret. We were actually in danger if we played it wrong.

"They just attacked!" A woman yelled at me. "Right off the tracks! Damndest thing I ever saw!"

"How did they attack?" I asked. This was the first group of people I had encountered who had seen the attack from beginning to end and they might have some valuable information.

Another man spoke up, a thin drink of water with a long scar on the side of his face. "They just ran through town, biting anyone they met. Crazy thing, they didn't stop to eat, just bite and run. If they couldn't get you right away, they ran off."

That was weird. "Anything else?" I asked.

Another woman yelled at us. "They took some of our kids! They just grabbed them and ran away! You have to get them back!"

I looked down. "Your kids are dead. These guys aren't taking kids for food; they're taking them for recruits."

Several people yelled at once, and one man walked forward, holding a length of lumber which was dark at one end.

"Damn you! Why weren't you here sooner? You could have stopped them with all your damn guns!" The man stepped up to about fifteen feet away when a shot from behind me split the air between us.

Charlie lowered his rifle slightly. "Let's try and stay friends, shall we?"

One look at Charlie in full gear changed the minds of several men who were beginning to walk forward. I hadn't even flinched when the shot was fired. I smiled to myself, and then changed the subject.

"We need to get moving if we have any chance of catching these zombies. Just let us know which way they went and at the least, we can avenge your dead," I said.

That set off another round of yelling, which was only interrupted by a low moan coming from the firehouse. I turned quickly and saw one of the wounded in the building come stumbling out. His arm was black from the virus, and he was pale from death. His dead eyes looked around and he uttered another moan.

Charlie was closest, so he just raised his rifle and shot the man in the head as he took another step forward. In the bay of the firehouse, several prone forms were beginning to twitch and stir.

"Excuse us for a moment," I said. Following Charlie, we walked the bay and efficiently put a rifle round through each of the people lying there. The biggest danger was a round ricocheting off the concrete and hitting us after passing through a zombie. We were careful to aim at an angle which kept the round away from us. It didn't help the back wall any, but that wasn't our lookout.

We finished our task and went back outside. The crowd had dispersed somewhat, but there were still several people milling about. They looked dazed, like they had fallen from a good height and had the wind knocked out of them.

"Can anyone tell me anything more about these zombies?" I asked the crowd in general.

A teenager stepped forward. He was about nineteen or less, and wore loose jeans with a plain white t-shirt.

"I could tell you where they're headed," The boy drawled slowly. He was armed with a long knife, the end of which was black and rusty.

"Which way?" I asked, getting into the truck.

"I said I could. Didn't say I would."

I looked at him for a moment. "Suit yourself."

We left him open-mouthed and his cohorts in a similar state behind as we drove south to get back to 34. Tommy radioed to Freeman what had happened, but was unable to get a response. I figured we needed to get west as quickly as possible. We were right behind these guys, but we had to detour a bit to get ahead of them. That was one of the problems with travelling by truck. We were limited to the roads while the little Z's could travel wherever. I wasn't about to go chasing them down on foot. Not that I was worried about meeting the zombies, but Sarah would shoot me dead for such a stupid idea.

CHAPTER 12

We reached the end of 164 and turned east again on 34. The countryside was heavily wooded, interspersed with farms and small ponds. There were no more large population centers the further we moved away from water, and I was grateful for that. We drove as quickly as we could, and Sarah pointed out to me that the next town on the map that connected with the railroad was Biggsville, and we might be able to set up an ambush there.

I looked at the map for a second and it made sense. We had covered the distance in about ten minutes, and with the small ten-minute head start the zombies had on us, we might just get a break with this one. The only thing that worried me was the possibility that the kids might leave the railroad and get around us. In that case, it was up to Colonel Freeman.

We reached Biggsville, and turned up S. Church Street, which seemed to be the main road through town. The first row of houses we passed showed no signs of any recent habitation, and the side roads we passed were full of homes falling into disrepair and ruin. The Illinois Department of Transportation building seemed to be in good shape, being made of brick, but the Biggsville United Presbyterian Church had one wall completely caved in, giving the building a grumpy frown.

Further north, the rows of houses ended at Arthur Street, and it was where the tracks passed through town. It was there I figured we needed to set our ambush.

I parked the truck on Church Street, backing it up to a small building that was built close to the street. Sarah got out and we both started filling our pockets with loaded magazines and ammunition. Charlie drove the van to the bridge and parked it on the top of the bridge overlooking the railroad. Sarah and I jogged over to the van as the rest of the crew was loading up. We took the time to put on our gloves, balaclavas, and goggles. This fight might get very close, and I wanted everyone to have as much protection as possible.

Duncan, in his usual way, had to have something different. His forearms were sheathed in leather greaves, which he had modified to accept a large nail. With those bad boys, he could punch through a zombie's head with little trouble. They did interfere somewhat with the swinging of his sword, but that was his trouble to figure out.

We mat at the van and I outlined the general plan. "We'll hit them with everything we have from the top of this bridge. We'll wait until they are on that little bridge there, so there is nowhere to go but forward or backward. If they get past that choke point, we'll let them come to us and we'll take them as they try and get to the bridge."

It wasn't complicated, and required little in the way of preparation. The only glitch would be the kids getting off the track early or coming from another direction. I had an uncomfortable thought that the kids had already passed us, or were going around us, but we had to try something.

Rebecca was standing on the van, using her riflescope to scan the surrounding area and look down the tracks. While she was up there, Charlie and I spoke in low tones, looking over the terrain and trying to figure out where we could hit them again after the initial shock. I motioned for Tommy and Duncan to go to the south side of the bridge, and fire from a lower position, driving the zombies back into the firing zone from the high part of the bridge. The creek ran along the north side of the tracks, so there wasn't anywhere for the zombies to go on that side.

If we were working with normal zombies, this wouldn't be necessary. They would just shuffle forward and trip consistently over their fallen comrades before it was their turn to get shot. But the zombies we were after were not what we were used to, and we were adapting to them as quickly as we could.

Charlie and I were alerted by Rebecca tapping her foot on the roof of the van. She was looking intently through her scope, and we knew she had seen something.

"They're coming!" She whispered.

I pulled my rifle around and set up on the side of the bridge, just south of the van. I put a spare magazine on the rail next to my gun, just to make reloads faster. Charlie stationed himself on the north side of the van, and Sarah quietly climbed up to the roof of the van and joined Rebecca, who just laid herself prone on the same roof.

I looked through the scope on my rifle and waited. The railroad bridge was just an opening through a small swath of forest, which reached around the town and stretched off to the north and east. The sun was just past its zenith, so there weren't many shadows on the ground. The trees were just beginning to turn, so the area was beginning to show a decent amount of color. Illinois wasn't known for its forests, but it did the best it could with the trees it had.

"Sarah? Rebecca?" I whispered.

"What?" I didn't know who answered.

"Wait until the first ten clear the bridge, then take them out. Charlie and I will clear the middle, and Duncan and Tommy can get the ones that run for cover," I said, barely audible in the breeze. I wanted to get them on this side of the water, because if they went back, we'd lose them in the brush and it would be twice as hard to hunt them down.

It took a long time for the kids to show up. Rebecca must have had a powerful scope on her rifle. Looking through my own scope, I could see the lead zombies heading through the opening in the brush that led over the water. The zombies walked single file, and the ones who had been bitten earliest led the way. They were grayer in color, with black circles around their eyes. They walked quickly, but I knew they were capable of much faster movement. Younger, fresher zombies were in the middle, and I felt a pang as I saw several that were Jake's age. They never had a chance to live.

I could almost hear Sarah and Rebecca count to themselves as the zombies crossed the bridge. Ten passed, then twenty, and I was getting nervous that they weren't going to fire, then I was getting more nervous because that was a larger group of zombies than I had expected to meet.

The air suddenly split above me with the sound of high-powered rifles. Rebecca and Sarah worked their bolts like professionals, and kept the rounds pumping into the zombies. The first five were dead and finished, and the rest stopped short at the sudden sound of gunfire. Charlie and I opened up next, firing quickly, since our guns were semi-autos. I put down six on my side, and Charlie put down four more on his side.

The zombies recovered quickly enough. Ten of them raced towards us, while ten more ran off the tracks towards the south.

Duncan and Tommy started firing, and the rest of us did, too. We put down six more before they vanished underneath us.

"Duncan, Tommy, get out of there, they're past us!" I shouted. I expected them to run towards us and take cover in the van while we drove around and finished off the zombies. What I didn't expect, was the two of them run south, directly away from safety, and setting up a collision course with the ten who left the tracks.

CHAPTER 13

Charlie noticed it, too. "Are you kidding me?" He said, more to himself than to me.

"Come on, we have to get the other ones first!" I ran over to the other side of the bridge, covered by Sarah on the van.

I looked over the side of the bridge and a small head looked back at me. Its tousled hair was matted and bloody, and the face was bloody as well. The lack of wounds told me the blood didn't belong to the zombie. The face snarled at me, and I put a round through it before it could duck away into the brush. I didn't see the other ones, so they were under there somewhere.

"Sarah! Take the van and back up Tommy and Duncan. Charlie and I will get these three!" I shouted. There was no point in whispering now.

"Got it! Be careful!" Sarah scrambled off the roof of the van and got in, slowly pulling off the bridge and heading out after the dynamic duo. Rebecca threw Charlie a small wave as she rode the roof to the rescue.

Charlie joined me on the side and used his rifle to guide his search as he looked over the side.

"Nothing here. Lot of brush over there, think they went that way?"

I shrugged. "Got to check. I'm going to walk wide, keep your rifle ready."

I took the long way, circling wide around the base of the bridge. Charlie leaned over the side of the bridge, keeping his rifle pointed at the ground. If a Z jumped out from there, they were going to get a round through the top of their head.

I moved carefully, trying to ignore the firing I heard from behind me. All it took was a second and these little bastards were up your ass. I stepped carefully around the base of the bridge and out into the open. A small line of trees and brush hid the railroad, so they could have been anywhere.

As I stepped further away from the bridge, I could see more and more of the area underneath it, and I didn't see anyone hiding there. I signaled to Charlie, who responded by running over to the far side of the bridge. A single shot later and a small form tumbled to the ground by a cluster of poison ivy vines.

That seemed to be a signal to the other two. They came running out of the brush, about fifteen feet apart. They were roughly the same age and same size, gender being the only real difference. The kids were very fast, and would hit me at exactly the same time.

Well, they would have if I let them. I lined up a shot and took out the girl, then fired at the boy. That shot would have killed him, but he jumped at the right time and the round hit him in the chest. Fortunately, it knocked him back several feet, and I used the slight hesitation between the recalibration of senses and the launching of offensives, to send a round through his confused face. The bullet penetrated his brain and dropped him without a fuss.

Charlie came sprinting over the bridge, and we both looked at each other as more firing came from the south. We ran down the main street, heading towards the truck I had parked there. At least we didn't have to run all over like last time.

Or so I thought. Just as we were crossing the last block to the truck, three zombies came tearing around the corner at us. I fired from the hip, missing completely, and Charlie fired from a low ready position, hitting one in the shoulder and the other in the chest, causing no damage at all. I tried to bring the rifle up, but it was too late, the zombie was on top of me. The barrel of my gun poked it in the forehead, and I fired again, missing as the zombies got knocked back and down from the impact of the muzzle.

Charlie was having issues of his own. His rifle was useless at this range, and more of a handicap than a help. He had pulled his 'hawks and was engaging his enemies with his preferred method of killing. A back swung right hand tomahawk took out a zombie that had re-engaged in the fight, and a left hand overhead chop wiped out the other one.

I stepped on the chest of the little boy who was struggling to get up and bite me in the leg, and using my own 'hawk, stuck a spike right between his dark eyes. I wiped my spike on the shirt of the zombie, and then realized that was a bad idea as blood smeared across the dark blade. I cursed silently and sunk the spike in the dirt, using the time-honored tradition of cleaning a blade of gunk and blood. I'd burn it later.

Charlie and I finished our run to the truck and hopped inside. Another shot took us south and back towards the Highway Building. We had no idea where the others were, we just had a vague reference based on the sound of shots.

We decided to circle around the far end of town, and work our way towards the middle. If we came charging in, we might find ourselves between the rifles of our friends and the zombies they were trying to shoot.

At the southern end of town, we were slowly moving west when a small zombie darted out from between two houses. Suddenly, a shot from over our shoulders took the zombie in the side, knocking her over into the grass. A second shot from another source took the zombie in the head, ending it.

I stopped the truck, understanding that we would just be in the way. Charlie and I got out and climbed into the bed of the truck, rifles at the ready. Clearly, there was some kind of hunt going on, and we were not invited.

After a minute, Duncan appeared, running out into the open, chased by two little boys intent on causing some damage. As he passed the two buildings, two shots took down the two Z's. Tommy was next, and he was cutting it close with an older boy and a younger girl. They were right on his heels, and if he stumbled, they certainly would get him. Two shots later, the danger seemed past.

"That it?" Charlie called out.

Duncan looked around, and counted swiftly. "That's all we have for this end. What about you guys?"

"Got the ones by the river, so we should be done," I said. "Anyone take a serious look at one of these?"

Tommy shook his head. "Nope. It's dead, and they're better deader."

I chuckled. "Good one. No, seriously."

"What are you seeing, John?" Sarah called from her rooftop.

"They're wet."

CHAPTER 14

Everyone looked. Sure enough, each one was soaking wet, like they had taken a dip in the local creek. I thought about it, and realized these guys just eliminated a barrier we had used for years. They didn't stay away from water.

"Damn," Duncan said. "Well, I'd bet the river by Starved Rock would keep them occupied."

"Wonder how they crossed?" Tommy asked out loud, something I was wondering myself.

"Right now, doesn't matter. We need to get in touch with Freeman and give him an update. We just took out a force of forty of the enemy, so that should be good news to him," I said.

"Finally, some good…" Charlie said, but he never got to finish. Right as he was saying that, ten little zombies burst out around the corner of a small house, its hedge grown to over five feet. We were caught out in the open, with nowhere to run, and unable to use our guns for fear of hitting each other. We had five seconds to do something.

"Back to back! Move! Sarah! Rebecca! Take whatever shots you get! Don't worry about us!" I yelled, dropping my rifle and pulling out my pickaxe. Charlie put his back facing mine and Duncan did the same with Tommy. We were protected from rear attacks as long as we kept our footing.

The first little bastard ran forward and I slammed my pickaxe into him. I missed him with the metal head, but the handle was seasoned hickory and it landed like a bat on his foul ball. The impact threw him sideways, and my return swing slammed into the ribs of a taller zombie, sweeping her hands away just inches from my face. I didn't try to hit them in the head, I was just trying to keep them away from me with the tools I had on hand. Behind me, Charlie was swinging hard, knocking down zombies and keeping them there.

Another zombie launched himself towards me, but a shot from the roof slammed him to the ground. The sound halted the rest for a brief second and I took the opportunity to bury the point end of my pick in a downed zombie's head.

Duncan was cutting a small zombie in half while Tommy was batting them out of the park as I was. He actually knocked one close enough to me to allow me to finish it off. We didn't often get assists, but it helped.

The last zombie kid squared off with Charlie, and it was interesting to see it work. It moved forward slowly, keeping an eye on Charlie's left hand tomahawk. Charlie flicked the blade forward, and the kid's eyes actually followed it. His mistake, since the other 'hawk was already moving and cracked his skull about three inches behind his eye. He never knew what killed him as he sank to the ground.

We straightened up and finished off our leftovers, keeping a wary eye on the surrounding houses and trees. Sarah and Rebecca scanned the area carefully and declared it safe. We pulled them down from the houses and spent a good amount of time cleaning our weapons.

"Close enough, that one," I said.

"Yeah, but I wish we could figure out how they were communicating," Charlie said. "That last group clearly was waiting for us to be off guard, and had we been closer to them, they would have gotten one of us."

"Zoosemiotics," Duncan said.

"Fly that one again?" Charlie said.

Duncan smiled. "Zoosemiotics. The signs animals give each other to communicate. Like 'play face' and tail wagging, when two dogs look like they're about to kill each other, but they're just playing."

Tommy shrugged. "I really just met him during the Upheaval."

I was intrigued. "Talk to me. How are they communicating?"

"If I had to guess, I would say they are using a combination of signals and sounds. Something more complex than the communication that goes on between higher order animals, but nothing as complex as an actual language," Duncan said.

Rebecca asked the obvious. "How do you know?"

Duncan smiled again. "Do you guys know that none of you ever asked me what I did before the Upheaval?"

I had to admit I was shocked. I thought I knew my friends, but this was actually a surprise and a little embarrassing. "I always figured you just did regular work like regular folks. You never talked about it."

"I worked for Brookfield Zoo as a researcher in animal behavior and analysis. I was an intern there, working on field research for my eventual thesis."

I didn't take a step back, but I think everyone else did. We always thought of Duncan as a screwball, but a good man and fighter. Never did we associate him with higher learning.

"Okay then. Well, you were saying?" I asked, wiping off my pick.

"These guys are communicating using crude gestures and sounds to convey meaning. I wouldn't doubt there is some kind of crude training that goes on for the new recruits. They have an overall objective, which is communicated, as in what commands to obey and when they should obey them. It's not a perfect system, thankfully, but it is what they have," Duncan said.

"So how smart would you say they are?" Sarah asked, clearly intrigued.

Duncan shrugged. "I'd say Rebecca was right on in her estimate that they are probably as smart as cats, with the leader being as smart as a good dog. They may have more subtle communication among themselves, but we can see that the general overall plan is to keep moving east. The leader, whoever she is, will likely be the smartest zombie we have ever come across. I would not be surprised if she could actually speak."

I nearly sat down at that one. Holy cow. The more I thought about it, the more I started to think I wanted to take her alive. But when I looked down at the bloodied and dead bodies of the small ones ripped from their homes and mothers, taken away by monsters? How much horror were the last few moments of their lives? No, I'll kill any of these I find. Period.

"All right, well, we're not getting any further ahead, and we've scored a major victory here. Let's see if we can catch the zombies between here and the army, and finish them off for good," I said.

Everyone agreed, and it was going to be a fantastic thing if we could finally finish this and go home.

Aboard the truck, Sarah asked me a simple question. "Feeling better about our chances?"

"I think we got this one, finally." I said. "I really do."

Sarah smiled. "Me, too. Thank God."
"Let's get moving."

CHAPTER 15

It took us a while to find a survivor. I really wasn't expecting anyone, but in the cab of a truck, huddled in a ball on the floor, was a live soldier. Tommy found him as we searched the remains of the battlefield for anything that might give us a clue as to what had happened.

Earlier in the day, we had taken on fifty of the little kids, a significant chunk of their forces, or so I had hoped. The rest seemed to be on a collision course with Freeman's line.

As the sun began its long descent, we had come up from route 34 and were south of Kirkwood when we found the line. There were bodies everywhere, some twitching with the virus, and some dead from self-inflicted wounds. Brass casings were all over the road, and I seriously didn't think we were going to find any extra ammo anywhere. Weapons were scattered and tossed. I could see from my vantage point that there were many soldiers out in the grass, run down by the zombies that never tired, and ran as fast as they did.

Sarah just shook her head, although I thought I caught a glisten of a tear in her eye. I didn't blame her. This was a damn mess.

I radioed to the other van and truck. "Let's head south and see if they got caught there as well. May as well see how big the cleanup will be."

We drove south, weaving around bodies, trucks, and other vehicles. I stopped every once in a while to check a truck, and we got lucky here and there with some extra ammunition. Tommy walked along the road and picked up weapons, chucking them into the back of the truck Duncan drove.

At the big bend of County Highway 11, just outside of Smithshire, we reached the end of the line. South of us there wasn't any more trucks, nor any more corpses. It seemed to me that hope was dying as quickly as the army was.

"Well, here we go," I said, climbing out of the truck. I pulled out my rifle and joined Charlie on the road. Sarah didn't get out, and I was intrigued when she slid into the driver's seat.

"I'm going to check the town for any help with the cleanup," she said as she drove away.

I shrugged and held up a fist to Charlie. "Ready?"

He nodded. "One, two, three...Dammit!"

I chuckled. "You nearly always pick rock, you dope."

"I like rocks, you paper sissy," Charlie said over his shoulder as he headed into the grass. His job, which we always contested over, was to go into the brush and get the zombies that had wandered off. We were fresh enough upon the scene that the dead weren't rising, but it was going to happen soon. I figured by the time we reached Kirkland, we'd be fighting the suckers head-on.

The road duty was easier, but messier. On the grass, blood seeped into the ground and didn't spread all over. On the road, it was harder to avoid. There was also the inevitable release of bodily wastes when death occurred, which amplified by a few hundred souls and I felt like I was walking through a toilet. I walked slowly, carefully putting a .223 round into the face of each soldier I encountered. Blood was everywhere, and some of the men had been brutally savaged. There were women here, too, as our new army didn't really care about your gender as long as you came to fight. Not many, but a few. A couple of the soldiers were face down, and I just put the barrel of my rifle at the base of their necks and fired upward. If it didn't hit the brain, it obliterated the spinal cord, which killed the zombie pretty well, too.

I checked the cab of the first truck I came across, and it was a bloody disaster. The soldier that was in there didn't have a face, but pieces of it were all over the dashboard. Blood covered the seats and windshield, and the torn throat of the soldier showed how rough this death was. I put a round into the empty eye socket and moved on.

Behind me, Charlie cursed as he scampered over the road, heading to the other side to check the bushes and tall grass. I didn't pay attention as I approached the next vehicle, but I could have sworn I heard the words 'goddamn paper,' as he slipped over the far ditch.

Five more corpses led me to a small car, and I got a surprise when I saw that the window seemed to have been smashed in with a rock. Sure enough, in the lap of a very surprised looking dead man, was a stone the size of a softball. *Wow. Using tools, too.* I thought to myself. This just keeps getting better. The soldiers that took refuge in the car had chewed up faces and hands. Defensive wounds against an enemy that came in right at you.

A shot from the east drew my attention and I could see Charlie making his way through a field. His work will be impossible in a short while, we'd have to leave it to Rebecca and Sarah.

Sarah came up from the south, leading a convoy of about ten cars. They ranged in style from pickup to minivan, but the people inside were of a single stripe. Survivors.

They pulled up to a stop behind the van, and Rebecca got out to greet them. Charlie was out in the field, but when he saw what was going on, he came over quickly enough.

Fifteen men and ten women greeted me, and I thought I saw a few familiar faces in the crowd. This was the group we should have had facing the zombies, not the new army.

"Hey," I said, as a way of greeting. I assumed Sarah had filled them in on most of the details, anyway.

A man stepped forward, a tough looking guy about my age, with an axe handle peeking over his shoulder. "Talon, right?" he said extending his hand.

"That's right."

"Turner Hass, from Smithshire. Your wife says we got some cleanup to do?"

I gestured with my hands. "This road is covered all the way to 34. Don't know about anything further north. The line was supposed to go to 116, but I think it got ended here."

"Damn," said Hass. "Where you need us?"

I thought for a minute. "You guys know the terrain around here better than we do. Why don't you take the countryside, and we'll take the road."

"Sounds good. Can we get some weapons off these soldiers?" Hass asked.

"Sure, but I'll save you a trip," I said as Tommy and Duncan came rolling up.

After introductions, I brought the group to the back of the truck, and Tommy had piled up dozens of rifles and magazines.

"Help yourself," I said.

Hass smiled and took the weapon Tommy offered him, along with a spare mag. The rest of the crew from Smithshire armed themselves similarly, and went off the road, looking for zombies.

Tommy gave me a glance, and I shrugged. "We've still got a bunch, what's twenty five out of a couple of hundred?"

Duncan spoke up. "Twelve percent. We gonna stand here all day?"

"Nope. You get in touch with Freeman?" I asked.

"I think we're out of range, but I'll try further north."

"All right, let's go."

Tommy joined me on the road with Charlie, while Sarah, Rebecca and Duncan drove the vehicles. It became a kind of routine. The first one to come upon a dead soldier would shoot it, and then the other two would drag it off the road. This continued for about two miles, and after that, it became impossible, since the dead were rising and not inclined to lie quietly until it was their turn to get shot.

It was about that time when the crew from Smithshire began to earn their way. One of them walked through the field, getting the zombies to follow them, and when they were bunched up following, two more would run forward with a length of rope, knocking the crowd down. The rest would step in and finish them off. It was efficient, and the ease with which they used it told me, they were very familiar with this practice.

About a mile from Kirkwood, we pulled up and called in the crew from Smithshire.

"Hey, Hass," I said, pronouncing it 'hoss', and the man grinned broadly.

"Hey, Talon. Thanks for the hardware," He said, cradling his rifle.

"You all earned the heck out of it," I said. "Let me do you another. That truck over there looks abandoned. Why don't you take it back with you? Saves you the walk back to your vehicles."

"Hey! Thanks, Talon." Hass held out his hand and I shook it. It seemed almost surreal, having this conversation while about a hundred zombies were converging on our position, but after the Upheaval, we tended to take these things in stride.

CHAPTER 16

Tommy went over to check the truck out, and that's when we found our survivor. He was tucked in the fetal position on the floor of the truck on the passenger side, his arms wrapped around his legs with his knees up by his chin. He was shivering, and his eyes were staring straight forward, seeing nothing.

I waved Tommy off and motioned Rebecca to come forward. Charlie was right behind her in case the situation turned south. Rebecca spoke in low tones to the man, trying to calm him down and bring him out of his shock.

Whatever was going through the man's head, he wasn't going to calm down at all. He started breathing hard, and then he covered his ears with his hands, blocking all sounds. His rocking became worse, and I knew he was about to explode. I waved the two of them off and walked over.

"*Soldier!*" I barked. "On your feet! *Move it! Move it! Move it!*" I figured if I couldn't break him out of his shock, we'd have to physically pull him out of the truck, and someone was going to get hurt.

"Sir!" The boy actually shook himself out of his state and tried to stand up, cracking his head on the dashboard. He rolled out of the truck and tried to get himself to attention while holding his head, but when he saw the massacre and the advancing zombies, he fell to his knees, and I was afraid he was going to relapse.

"*Get on your goddamn feet*! No one told you take a nap! *Get up!*" I yelled again, using my across-the-playground Principal's voice.

The soldier stood and I got in his face. "What the fuck happened here, soldier? Don't waste my goddamn time with bullshit. You have one fucking minute, or I will gouge out your eyeballs and hang them from my mirror!"

Somehow, that worked. The soldier told his story quickly while Hass and his townspeople loaded up the truck and headed away, throwing waves to the rest of my crew and swerving around oncoming hordes of zombies.

"Sir. They came at us from the southern end, attacking everyone. The men from the line at 116 tried to come to help, but they got overrun. Everyone just shot bullets everywhere and died. They smashed windows to get us. They tore us apart."

The soldier's eyes misted with memories and I let him alone for a minute.

"How many?" I asked, using a gentler tone.

"I don't know." The soldier hung his head.

"Take a good guess, how many would you say there were?"

"I don't know! I just ran and ran and ran. People were screaming and dying, running into the grass, trying to escape. I don't know!"

"Soldier, we're about to be attacked in ten minutes, and I need to know how many. Take your best guess, then I'll let you run away again," I said.

The boy closed his eyes, and I could see he was working through his memories, trying to sort out a number.

"There was at least a hundred, maybe a hundred and fifty," he said finally.

Jesus. "Okay soldier. Take off. I think you'll find Freeman at Kirkwood to the north."

Without another word, and with no attempt to retrieve a weapon, the soldier just bolted up the road.

"Nice work," said Charlie. "You sounded like someone we knew."

"Yeah," I said. "But we'll have to stop Nate from killing him for cowardice."

"True."

"John?" Tommy asked as he lined up a shot on an advancing zombie.

"Yeah?"

"We gonna fight, or what?"

I went to the truck. "No."

Duncan paused in pulling out his sword. "What are we going to do with these guys, then?"

"Bring them with us. Mount up," I said, winking at Sarah.

Sarah just shook her head at me, but smiled when I kissed her. "Thanks for bringing the best of Smithshire."

"No problem. They looked bored when I rolled up, and were happy to help out."

"Well, they did, so now we can get rolling," I said.

"All right. What about the zombies?"

"Just drive north, but not too fast," I replied.

Sarah got it instantly. "Army's problem."

"Army's mess. It's time Freeman cleaned up his own."

"I fully agree." Sarah pulled forward, but stayed at a speed of about five miles and hour. Immediately, Rebecca pulled in behind, staying close. Duncan had a bit of a difficulty getting his truck started, which allowed a couple of soldier zombies the opportunity to grab on to the mirrors, but once he got rolling, they fell off quickly enough.

The town of Kirkwood was a big place, and like several places of its size after the Upheaval, found it was difficult to take care of all the people it housed. So the town was actually populated by about half of its former three thousand, and the rest had gone to other communities, bolstering their defenses and contributing what they could. Eventually the city would return to its former size, but they just didn't have the resources yet.

We crested a small hill and saw a line of soldiers facing us. They were standing by their vehicles, which had been parked sideways across the road. Right away, I knew we were going to have trouble. I told Sarah to speed it up so we could get better defenses prepared.

We pulled up to the trucks and I got out, waving a soldier over.

"Where's Colonel Freeman?" I asked.

"Back at the command post, sir," The soldier, a kid, little older than twenty, answered nervously.

"Better go get him, son. You're about to be attacked," I said. The boy ran off, and I went over to the milling men.

"Listen up! These trucks need to be off the road, I need three on the east side, three on the west side. Angle them all so they're facing southwest-northeast, and put them about ten feet apart. Move now!" I yelled.

Thankfully, the men were ready to listen. They must have heard the shots from the south, but their vision was obscured by the small hills. Those small hills probably saved their lives, because the little zombies would have taken their rampage right into the heart of Kirkwood, and we'd have lost the rest of the damn army.

As the last truck was being put in place, Tommy and Duncan were organizing the men into firing squads, three groups of five. One group would fire until they were empty, then the next group would advance up to the firing line, while the first went back to reload. The trucks were angled to prevent the men from shooting each other, and a large opening down the middle would allow for firing from the front. It was the best we could do for troops not used to zombies and with a short amount of time.

"Talon!" Colonel Freeman's voice cut across the road. "Thank God, you're alive!"

"Colonel," I said, waiting for the man to reach me.

"What's going on, why are these men being deployed, have you heard from my troops to the south? We heard firing, but felt it was better to maintain our position and protect the people of Kirkwood."

"Your men are being deployed to handle the threat of zombies; yes, I have heard from your troops to the south, and by the way, here they come now."

CHAPTER 17

The first group of zombies came into view as they shuffled their way over the hill. No one could mistake them for living, the slow gait and low moan marked them as undead even to people unfamiliar with them. Some of their helmets were skewed and covering an eye, while others were dark with blood. One had no face left, and another was drooling a dark liquid on the ground.

I walked away from Colonel Freeman, who was frozen in horror, and stood in the middle of the trucks. "Hey! Right here! Hi guys!" I was more worried about some nervous nitwit shooting me in the back, than the hundred or so zombies on the way.

The zombies responded warmly and shuffled quickly in my direction. Actually, I think they were just moving downhill as opposed to wanting to make a new friend. I waited until the number of zombies reached about fifty, and then I went back to Freeman.

"The rest of your men are dead, killed by the little zombies and finished off by us and some friends from Smithshire. You need to figure out what you are going to do with the rest of your men, because unless you do something right, you're going to get them all killed, and leave everyone in those zombie's path defenseless." I was harsh but honest. Freeman wasn't a fool, and he did what he could with what he had, but he was outgunned with this one.

Freeman watched the zombies come forward. Sarah and Rebecca were keeping the men in the main road from firing, and Tommy, Duncan and Charlie were waiting with their groups to open fire. If it all worked to plan, we'd be done here in about fifteen minutes.

"What are you going to do?" Freeman asked.

"I'm going home to batten down the hatches. I know what I'm facing and know how I need to prepare. I have a family that might be in danger right now, and I need to get home." I looked at the sky, and the sun was about two hours away from setting. I did not want to spend another day away from home, and I was tired of sleeping in the truck.

"Talon. This is the hardest thing for me to admit, but I don't know what to do." Freeman looked at me for a moment, and then looked down.

I sympathized with the man. I knew what it was like to be the one everyone looked to for answers, and the pressure put on a leader was immense. We always questioned ourselves, always wondered if we were doing the right thing, praying for miracles, readying our excuses for failure. Sometimes, all we wanted was to be the one looking for the answer, not the one expected to provide it.

I looked around; making sure no one could hear us. "You can't fight them head on, this mess proves it. Do the next best thing, get your men ahead of them, and warn the communities. Let them know what they're facing. There's enough veterans of the zombie wars out there that they'll know what to do. Hell, they might take out a few for you. But they have to know about the threat. Go tell them, and do it as quickly as possible. You're running short on time. The ones who caused this massacre are likely three miles away by now. You'll probably never catch them in the open, but you can ambush the shit out of them with everyone watching where they go. That's your best option."

Freeman opened his mouth to answer, but the first crash of rifles interrupted him. Fifteen zombies dropped, and then the killing began. The horde got it from the sides and from the front. In a short amount of time, the road was strewn with dead again bodies. There was a bit of commotion as some soldiers broke down after killing friends, but it was handled by Charlie and Tommy.

I looked at Freeman. "Get this cleared, and then get away. You know what to do. Break your men into groups of ten, and use every vehicle you have. You'll have to take every road you can see, and check all the communities from here to Chicago. But you have to get it done now."

Freeman nodded, and I waved a hand to get my crew back together. We regrouped at the trucks, and within twenty minutes, we were on our way. I told Sarah about what I had told Freeman and she agreed completely. I then spent about fifteen minutes looking over the map, trying to put together some kind of path that the kids were following.

The only thing I could put together at the moment, was that they were travelling in a kind of north-northeast direction, which given the attacks we just saw and the sparing of Kirkwood, I'd say Monmouth was not likely to get hit, being further north. The only town of any size in the way was Galesburg, and Freeman would be on his way there. I didn't think he'd make it in time, and I said so to Sarah.

"What's the plan, then?" Sarah asked as she drove without direction.

"Stay on 34 until it breaks north to Monmouth, check in with them, and then head east. There a tiny town right in the way of these zombies, if they're still headed the way I think they are. If anyone's there, they'll be dead in short order." I said.

"You got it."

I relayed the plan to the van, and Charlie brought up a good point. He wanted to know where we were going to hunker down for the night. I told him we had to warn Cameron, the town in the way, and after that, we could bed down for a few hours.

CHAPTER 18

Sarah pushed the truck as fast as she could, hoping to get ahead of the zombies to Cameron. It was only about ten miles, and I hoped the landscape would slow down our little friends to give us enough time to catch up. I would welcome another chance at the horde, and if we could do some serious damage, we could slow the threat down to manageable levels.

We passed Monmouth in a short time, and paused only to send in a message. Monmouth was a decent town, and the people there had decided on a unique approach to the zombie problem early on. Instead of building defenses, they dug them. Monmouth had two main roads that went right down the center of town, dividing it into four equal parts. In addition, there was a road for each border of the town. The people of Monmouth just took their trackers and earthmovers, and dug up the roads. Then they just kept digging, eventually making the trenches about fifteen feet deep. After that, they simply put up some barricades to keep themselves from falling in, and went about their lives. There was a single drawbridge to get into the town, and it was manned at all times by a couple of very serious looking men with scoped rifles. We gave our message to them and they promised to pass it along and make sure they were ready. I didn't worry too much about the birthplace of Wyatt Earp.

We took 180th Avenue all the way to Cameron, and it was almost disappointing to have no one there to warn. We knew we were ahead of the zombies, but without actually seeing them, we'd only be guessing as to where they were. The town was quiet, and as the sun was casting long shadows over the land, I knew it was time to pack it in for the night.

"See if you can find someplace secure," I said, looking once more at the map.

"Will do. You want someplace high?" Sarah asked.

"If you can find one, that'd be great. I don't see anything we could use, though."

"A little faith, Mr. Talon."

If she saw something I didn't, I was more than willing to go along. My head was heavy and I just wanted to curl up into a little ball and sleep. I was consoled by the notion that we should be home by tomorrow evening and I would be back with my sons. This trip had been so much longer than I had anticipated, and I was going to owe my brother a lot for watching the kids as long as he had.

Sarah pulled up Highway 5 and turned onto Church Street. Two blocks up and there was the structure I was looking for. I wasn't able to see it from the ground, but somehow Sarah had.

"Well done, Mrs. Talon. Very well done," I said, giving Sarah's leg a small squeeze.

"You can appropriately thank me another time," Sarah said, picking up my hand and giving it a small kiss.

I walked around the grain silos and saw they were well placed to keep us safe. At the top of one of the silos was a control booth, and it looked big enough to sleep about four of us. That was the good news. The not-so-good news was that two of us would have to sleep in the van or truck.

The rest of the crew stretched out of the van and we took a minute to walk around the silos. Charlie gave the structure a thumbs-up, and even managed a grin when Rebecca pointed out the shack on top.

"Dibs," was all he said.

I laughed. "Let's get our stuff and get up there, all of us. I don't know when or where our friends are, but I'd rather be up there and unseen as soon as possible."

We climbed up the silo, and there was a small platform around the booth that allowed us some more room. A walkway stretched out to the other silo, and ended in another small platform. I had to admit, when Sarah picked them, she sure did a great job.

The booth was just a small control center, with a series of switches and dials on one wall. There was a table, a chair, and a small broom. The floor was rubber, likely to avoid static buildup. Charlie took the furniture out and carried it to the other platform. When I looked at him funny, he just shrugged.

"Whoever sleeps over there would probably like a little protection from the rain that's coming," Charlie said, pointing to the dark clouds just peeking under the setting sun.

"Good point. Maybe we can all fit in the booth," I said.

"Think they're heading this way?" Charlie wanted to know.

"No idea for sure, just a hunch, but they seem to be travelling in this direction, for whatever reason," I replied.

"You check the map for their possible destinations?" Charlie seemed to want a confirmation of what he had seen on the maps he had looked at.

I looked around and saw that no one else was near. "Yeah, and we need to get home as soon as we can. If they stay on this course, they're going to run dead on into Starved Rock."

CHAPTER 19

We didn't say anything after that, and just settled in for the night. The booth was a tight little box, and Duncan and Tommy elected to go sleep on the other end of the platform. They liked sleeping outdoors, so that was fine with me. A breeze was picking up, and we could smell rain in the air. Fortunately, the windows angled out and down, so we could keep them open even in a rainstorm.

We all crashed hard, and the only thing that woke me up was the sudden rush of wind and rain that came in the middle of the night. Tommy and Duncan moved in the night to the far side of the booth to get out of the rain, and all was well for a while.

It must have been around two or three in the morning when I woke up. I don't know what caused me to be suddenly wide awake, but when I glanced over at Charlie, I saw he was awake as well. He nodded towards the outside, and I disentangled myself from Sarah to get up and outside.

The rain had stopped, and the night was full of that fresh-washed, earthy smell that gave a sense of renewal no matter where you were. The wind was slower, but there was still a good breeze from the west. Charlie and I walked out to the platform on the other silo, and I took the chair while he sat on the table.

"What woke you up?" I whispered.

"Just a feeling," Charlie said. "Just a feeling."

"Yeah, me too."

We didn't speak after that, and it was a good thing, because suddenly, they were here. One moment, the night was quiet and dark, and everything was where it was supposed to be. The next moment, shadows were flowing around buildings, going into homes, checking out garages. From where we were, we could see several glowing eyes moving through the night like malignant fireflies that never blinked. They moved so fast and were upon the town so sudden, if there was anyone down there; they were dead before they knew it.

This was how they attacked towns. Waiting until they were all in position, and then running through without stopping. It explained why town after town fell, why they were able to be so effective. I watched them climb fences and flow up stairs without a second's hesitation. The eerie part was the pace. Every single one of them moved at exactly the same speed. It was a fast walk, a quick search, and then on. There was a brief flurry of movement as an animal was disturbed out of its nest, but a squeal was all that remained of that critter.

The shadows flowed towards the silos, and Charlie and I simply froze. If anyone looked up, we would be part of the scenery, hidden against a dark sky. If anyone else from our group made a sound, however, we were all dead.

Charlie watched the flow, and his hand strayed to his firearm, but I shook my head as slightly as I dared. I understood his rationale, but we were limited in the ammo and the supplies we had with us.

The zombie kids kept moving, and in about thirty minutes, had faded into the surrounding brush. I waited another ten before I spoke, and even then, it was barely a whisper.

"The town is about a half mile in size, which means they are travelling at about two miles an hour. That gives us a good clue as to where they are going to be in the morning," I said.

Charlie watched the dark spot where the kids disappeared. "Why couldn't we have had our fight here? They couldn't get us."

"Yeah, but what happens when we run out of ammo or water? I forgot to set up a cistern for rain. Did you?" I asked, moving quietly back to the shack.

Charlie chuckled. "As a matter of fact, I did forget."

We reached the shack and settled back down with our spouses, who never knew we had left, to try and get a couple more hours of sleep. Strangely, I didn't dream of anything weird.

CHAPTER 20

In the morning, we quickly got off the tower and back to our vehicles. If the little Z's heard us or decided to double back for any reason, we needed to be mobile and not trapped up in the air.

I checked the map, and figured the zombies were headed towards Galesburg. Ordinarily, that would be a worry, but Galesburg was as dead as the day is long. A major highway runs alongside it, and a lot of fleeing, infected people were around Galesburg in the bad years. People from the east and north converged on the town, and it became a nightmare of blood and death. Even now, I never considered the town completely clear, even though we had been through it several times. There were a lot of places for zombies to hide, and the hordes that travelled the country could easily have gone to ground in a place like Galesburg.

"Stay on 34, we'll try and take it around Galesburg," I told Sarah as we pulled out of Cameron.

"Ugh. *The* Galesburg?" She said. Sarah hated the place.

"That's the one," I said.

"Think the body is still there?" She asked.

I hadn't thought about it in years. "Maybe." The mention of the body brought back a bad memory. When we were going from town to town and cleaned out zombies wherever we found them, a couple of men joined us. They were called Ben and Tim, and from the start, they were trouble. Ben was a white-haired man about ten years my senior, and Tim was a younger man with the same whitish hair.

Tim was forever trying to seduce the women that travelled with us, and even a stern talking to by Sarah didn't have any effect. He basically told her to mind her own business unless she wanted some of his. Sarah put him on the ground for that, and I stepped in later to tell him in no uncertain terms, what I would do to him with my knife if he ever spoke to my wife like that again.

That seemed to do the trick, but then we started to notice things were getting sloppy. Doors we thought we had locked were opened, weapons were not where we had left them, and in general, we were being set up to have a catastrophic failure which would get a lot of us killed.

Charlie finally caught Ben and his brother trying to sabotage some of our ammo, and that was the last straw. We held a quick trial, and banished the brothers from our group, never to return on pain of death.

That worked for a time, and we didn't see hide or white hair of either brother until Galesburg. During a heavy fight, Tim popped out of a store and grabbed one of our female fighters, dragging her inside and trying to rape her at gunpoint. She stuck a knife in his side and escaped, leaving him to our justice. He tried to fight, but Charlie overwhelmed him and that was that. I personally tied the noose around his neck and hung him from a streetlamp. Duncan was the one who put the 'rapist' sign around the dead man's neck.

We never saw Ben again, and I always wondered what had happened to that sneaking son of a bitch. I figured him for dead.

We drove slowly around Galesburg, and I saw a lot of places where we had fought. I saw the factory where Duncan nearly died, and the alleyway that saved all of our lives at one point. Tommy radioed in with his memories, and I had to say I was not unhappy to put Galesburg behind us.

At the north end, Sarah pointed to a light. "Well, I'll be damned."

I looked, and although I expected to see a corpse, what I saw was better. Swinging in the wind, like a tethered ball, was a skull on the end of a rope. The rest of the body either must have fallen away, or was pulled down by predators. Part of me wondered if Ben ever came back and tried to bury his brother, but didn't have a ladder so he had to make do with the parts he had.

We crossed Interstate 74, and could see the lines of rusting cars stretching away to the north and west. If we bothered to take 74, we would be days away from home, and that wasn't going to happen. We needed to get along the path to get in the way of the zombies, and I was hoping a great deal that they were delayed in Galesburg. I didn't see any sign of them, but that sure as hell didn't mean they weren't there.

The next town on our route was Wataga, and I had a good feeling that there were people there. The town was far enough away from 74 to not be a place for fleeing people, and there wasn't any exit from 74 in this area anyway.

Route 34 took us to the west side of town, and we pulled over at Casey's General Store. I didn't see anyone about, but the town looked tidy, and the mowed lawns told me *someone* was living here. I got out and stretched, and joined the rest of the crew in taking a little stroll to the general store. In the better times, it was a typical place to get supplies for the road, gas and such. If your beef jerky supply was low, this was the place to stock up.

Duncan and Tommy took a quick look into the store, and shook their heads when they exited.

"It's stocked, somewhat, so somebody was running the place. But there's no one here," Tommy said.

Charlie looked around and went over to the road that led into town. "I'm not seeing any activity, and I doubt they all decided to sleep in today."

"Make ready," I said, and at those words, everyone broke into action. Rifles were pulled out and magazines were checked. Knives and 'hawks were loosened in their sheaths, and guns were eased in their holsters.

"Let's split up. Sarah, you're with me and Duncan. Tommy, you're with Charlie and Rebecca. Swing to the north, and then slow walk to the south. We'll take the south-north route and meet you in the middle. If they're in hiding, call out as you walk, let them see you. If they're friendly, they'll come out," I said, patting myself for mags and knives.

"And if they aren't friendly?" Tommy asked.

"Try not to get killed," I said. "Let's go."

We got back in our vehicles and I drove to the southern end of town, parking on a street appropriately named East South Street. We radioed to Charlie that we would be walking down Simmons Street, and if he cared to join us, that's where we'd be. Charlie replied he'd be delighted. He reminded me that we needed to be quick. If the little zombies were on their way, the middle of a street wasn't the best defensible place.

"On our way," I said.

We got out of the truck and moved fast, checking houses and streets. It was eerie, walking through places that looked lived in, but no one was home. In one house, we found the remains of breakfast, and Sarah commented that the eggs weren't that cold. I looked out back and saw the chickens were just fine, getting in the morning pecks before getting down to the business.

I went into one house that looked to be occupied, and found no one. I even checked the upstairs bedroom and found no one there, either.

I checked in with Sarah, who was emerging from another house, and she found nothing out of sorts.

"Everything okay?" I asked.

"Yes and no," She said.

"Meaning?"

"Yes, everything is where is should be, as if a family decided to take a morning stroll, but no, there's no sign of struggle, no blood splatter, nothing."

I watched as Duncan came out of another house. "So there's no reason these houses should be empty."

"That's exactly what's wrong," Sarah concluded.

CHAPTER 21

We walked up the road, passing Coal Street, and made our way up to Willard. In front of us, I could see Charlie and Rebecca come out of a house looking baffled, and Tommy came out of another house, shaking his head. I could imagine their conversation was very similar to what we had been discussing.

We crossed Willard Street, and waited for the rest to meet us. I couldn't make heads or tails of what had happened to this town, but we didn't need to figure it out, we just needed to get moving if there was nothing here.

"What do you think?" I asked Charlie. I trusted his instincts better than I trusted my own, and wondered what he thought.

Charlie thought for a minute. "I'd say this town either saw them coming and they're up in their attics, or they got completely swept away and they're out in the weeds somewhere."

I had to agree, this was just way out of the ordinary. "All right, since there's nothing we could do here, let's get back to our vehicles and get moving."

"Duncan!" Tommy called. "Let's go!"

Duncan was walking up Willard Street, heading towards the Wataga Congregational Church. It was a low building, shaped in a large 'L'. Duncan was walking on the sidewalk, studying the building with an intensity that was raising the red flags.

I started walking in the same direction, and Charlie followed. Tommy pulled Sarah and Rebecca back to get the van, and I could hear their footsteps retreating quickly in the distance. They would be able to provide an escape if we needed it, but they had to get to it first.

Duncan reached the building, and I could see him carefully trying to look into the windows. They were casement windows, so they needed a crank to open them, and if there was trouble inside, I doubted any zombies would be able to figure it out. As I got closer, I could see the windows had been reinforced from the inside, and I figured out where everyone had gone. This town used the centermost building as a defense center. In case of attack, everyone retreated to this location, and they set up a coordinated defense. It made a lot of sense, and should have worked.

I walked around the opposite direction of Duncan, and tried looking in the windows as well. I could see that there was some reinforcing wood that was put up on the inside, and would be impossible for zombies to pull it out.

I stepped into the parking lot on the west side. There was a door on the south side, but it was locked. I put my ear to it and tapped, but didn't get a response. I thought I heard a tapping in return, but it could have been Charlie as he came around the corner.

We walked together to the front of the building, and stopped dead. Duncan was sitting in front of the open doors, his head in his hands, and I thought he was actually crying. Charlie and I stepped to where we could see, and our shoulders slumped as we looked into the church.

Bodies and body parts were everywhere, covering the floor and partway up the walls. Blood was absolutely everywhere, covering the small pews and altar. Men were torn to pieces and covered smaller bodies that they had tried to protect. The ceiling was decorated in blood spray, and a woman's body was near the altar, one arm outstretched, and holding on to the small hand of a child that was missing a head. Deeper into the building, we could see additional carnage, and none of it was good. This town had run for safety, but couldn't outrun the evil that pursued them.

Duncan stood up, and I could see he was extremely upset. I knew what was bothering him, and I put a hand on his shoulder.

"We're going home. This won't happen to our families," I said.

That seemed to calm him down, and he took several deep breaths to get himself under control. Charlie flipped on his flashlight, and stepped in the door a few feet to survey the damage.

He moved out again and whistled. "They're slaughtered completely. I'm not sure too many of them could come back."

I shook my head. "The blood is still flowing on the walls. This happened within the last hour. Did you see any sign of passage on the north side?"

Charlie shook his head. "Wasn't looking for any, but after what we saw last night, that many zombies would leave a huge trail an idiot could pick up."

"I agree. But we're back to square one. Let's torch this church and get moving. I think we need to get home as quickly as we can and see to our own defenses." As I said this, the van came slowly down the street. Rebecca was driving, and Tommy was sitting on the roof with his rifle up and ready. When they turned the corner and were able to see inside the church, their face fell, and Rebecca held one hand to her mouth.

Duncan went to the back of the van and pulled out a bottle of kerosene. He sprayed in inside the church and up on the wooden parts of the structure. He used half the bottle, and when he was finished, he tossed a single match, sending the poor souls of Wataga up to heaven on smoke trails.

I signaled to the van. "We'll stay here, and make sure this thing goes up right. Go grab the truck and meet us back here," I said. Rebecca nodded and Sarah gave me a small smile.

The three of us stood in the parking lot, and watched the flames spread over the church and start working on the roof. The flames were mostly quiet, and the windows hadn't blown yet, but they would soon.

If they had, we would have been killed. As it was, it was quiet enough for us to hear the little zombies as they attacked.

Duncan heard them first, a small noise coming from a house. He just turned his head and suddenly yelled out. "Here they come!"

I spun around, and in an instant, realized I couldn't use my rifle. The little Z's were moving too fast, and by the time I tracked them for a killing shot, they'd be too close. I whipped out my pickaxe and trench hawk, and waited for them to come. Charlie had his 'hawks ready, and Duncan was taking a two handed grip on the sword he had unsheathed.

Suddenly, I was mad. Deep, hardcore mad. I was tired of chasing these fuckers, tired of cleaning up after them, tired of being late to their slaughter, and tired of worrying about my family at Starved Rock. I bared my teeth and gripped my weapons in anticipation. I let my anger wash over me, flowing into my arms and hands. I wanted a fight, needed it, and delightfully, here it was.

Twenty of the monsters threw themselves at us and I charged them as they came within range. That threw them off, and several of them came up short as they tried to process this change. I didn't give them the chance to figure out what had happened, I waded in and cracked skulls left and right. I threw bodies away from me and punched the spike end of my hawk into little heads. I felt a pressure on my leg and looked down to see a small girl trying to chew into my calf. My pants were of a thick enough material that she couldn't bite through it, but she was sure working the hell out of it. I reached down, grabbed her by the back of the neck, and hauled her off her feet. I took a step forward and literally threw her over a fence and into a nearby house.

Suddenly I laughed. Charlie killed another one and yelled at me while Duncan wiped out two with a single swing of his sword. "What the hell is so funny?"

"They're just kids! They're not super strong and they don't weigh much more than dogs! There's nothing to fear!" I motioned to the remaining zombies, who milled just out of reach. "You want to fight, you little shits? It's time you feared *me*!" I charged again and swung my pickaxe like a bat. I took three with that move and smashed my 'hawk into another. "Come on!"

Charlie laughed at me and grabbed a little boy that had gotten to close. He held it by the neck and then threw it away from him. It hit the side of the church with a satisfying crack, and slumped down motionless.

It felt good to be on the offensive, and to be without fear. They couldn't get through my gear, and as long as I kept swinging and stayed on my feet, they had no chance. They weren't as strong as adult zombies, and they might have been fast, but I didn't plan on running anywhere.

Duncan was far more deadly with his sword, and bits of little zombies flew all over. I watched him for a second and figured that would be a good thing for him to teach my sons. Eventually the bullets would run out, and having skill with a three-foot knife wouldn't hurt.

Suddenly, the attack broke off. The little Z's turned and ran into the homes, away from us and angling away to the north. I picked up my rifle and shot down two of them, and Charlie bagged four. Two more were gunned down by Tommy, and that left the total for this fight at a little over twenty.

I squatted down, and hung my head between my knees. I was exhausted, and the adrenaline rush from the attack was wearing off, washing out of me like someone turned open a spigot in my foot. No matter what the hotheads say, fighting wears me out.

Charlie and Duncan came over, wiping off their weapons.

"You okay? They get you?" Charlie asked, worried.

I shook my head. "Just getting old, that's all." I stood up and walked over to the burning church, and stuck my weapons in the flames that came out of the window. When the red burned out, I wiped them off and put them back where they belonged. Duncan and Charlie did the same, and I had to admit the burning sword looked pretty damn cool.

Sarah and Rebecca came out to us, and Sarah surprised me once by jumping up and wrapping her arms and legs around me. I held her tight, and she whispered in my ear.

"You scared the shit out of me! What were you thinking, charging those monsters?" She said, gripping me tighter.

I chuckled. "I suddenly realized I wasn't afraid of them. I could handle this group, and they were just little kids."

Sarah pulled back and her eyes were wet. "Please don't do that again. I mean it."

I looked at her seriously. "Can't promise, but I'll try." I put her down and she wiped off her eyes. I had to admit, Sarah's discomfort worried me more than facing that horde of zombies. I'd have to think about this one a little bit.

"What's the plan, boss man?" Tommy said as he slid off the roof of the van.

I shrugged. "Let's try and get home as quick as we can. This delay cost us an hour we didn't have, and I don't want to be delayed any more. Cut a trail to home and get there."

"Amen, brother," Charlie said.

Duncan and Tommy piled into the van, and Charlie followed. Rebecca accosted Charlie the same way Sarah had me, and I could imagine the conversation they were having.

Inside the truck, Sarah held my hand and sat as close as she could.

"What's up, babe?" I said, pulling out of the town.

"I'm scared, John. I don't know why, but I'm scared," she said.

"Everything will be fine. When people know what's out there, they'll take care of it. We just have to have faith that Colonel Freeman is doing his job."

"Just get me home, John Talon."

"Yes, ma'am."

If I was worried before, I was downright terrified now. *Freeman, if you fail, you'll wish the zombies got you.* I thought.

CHAPTER 22

"Talk to me, Tommy."

"I'm not getting anything from anyone. I know we set these people up with communication, but I can't raise anyone."

"Keep trying. Let me know if you get in touch with anyone. Have you heard at all from Freeman or anyone with the army?" I asked, weaving around a fallen tree in the road.

"Not yet. I'll keep trying. Tommy out."

I looked over at Sarah and the worry was starting to show on her face. We made decent time out of Wataga, but then a fall storm came up and we had to wait it out under a viaduct. It was one of those horizontal rainstorms, and since we were travelling mostly country roads, the likelihood of us sliding into a ditch was too good to risk. So we waited out the storm and we were just getting underway, having lost another two hours of time. The sky was still grey with menacing rain, but for the time being, it had let up enough for us to move again. I doubted the zombies could move quickly in that downpour, so they likely didn't get very far.

I was concerned about the lack of communication. We should have been able to raise somebody; we were close enough to a couple of communities that I knew were active, but perhaps the storm knocked out a few comm centers. I just didn't know.

Oneida had been wiped out, but Altona had survived, having been visited by a group of soldiers the evening before. They didn't do anything special but lock their doors and windows and stayed inside until the danger passed.

Galva had been hit this morning, and they were cleaning up their friends and neighbors when we arrived. The situation looked to be the same. The zombie kids swarmed in, attacked who they could, carried off who they could, and disappeared before the defenses could be set. Tommy had to punch out a man who grabbed his shirt and started screaming in his face, and I had to draw my sidearm to keep the situation from getting worse. I was curious as to why the soldiers hadn't been here to warn them, but got the answer when the town leader told me a couple of their farmers found some dead soldiers about five miles from town. Freeman was late, again.

At around noon, we reached the town of Kewanee, and at first, it looked like we were going to have a situation like we did with Wataga. But on the north side, Charlie spotted something, and we drove north on 78 until we reached Johnson Sauk Trail State Park.

The park was heavily wooded, even more so since no one had been working to keep it back in its boundaries for several years. The trees had extended their growth, and the weeds had reclaimed large tracts of land on the southern end of the park. East State Road proved no barrier to the wilderness, and I suspected in about twenty years, the former state park was going to become a national forest.

We were greeted at the entrance to the park, which was a small road that dipped slightly before going up a small rise. Hills of tough scrub surrounded us as we made our way carefully to the barricade that stretched across the road.

"You Talon?" A burly man called out from the other side of the fifty-gallon drums that blocked the entrance.

"That I be. Who am I talking to?" I called back.

"Francis. Jerry Francis. Is it safe to head back to Kewanee?" A stocky man stepped out of the woods, cradling a long-barreled lever action. I'd guess that gun had a history with Jerry's family, and in all likelihood, the man could probably shoot extremely well with it.

"We just passed through there, and didn't see any sign of the zombies, so I'd say you were safe. Just to be extra careful, I'd post a watch on the southern end for a few days, and everyone should stay closer to home," I advised.

"Obliged to you. We'll head back this afternoon," Francis said.

"If you're heading back, may I make a suggestion?" I asked.

"Please."

"Just send a small group ahead, well-armed. Let them set up the first watch and then bring everyone back. You don't want to get hit as you just get back to town." I said.

Jerry mulled it over. "Good thought. We'll get it done. Thanks."

I reached across the barrier and shook his hand. "Stay safe."

Jerry smiled. "If you're chasing these ghosts, you do the same."

"Done."

We turned our trucks around and headed back south, turning off Route 34 and following Kentville Road. Tommy told us that Neponset hadn't been hit, and they had been in contact with Scheffield and Buda, and those towns had been warned by the military. Sarah crossed them off the map, which put our enemy somewhere to the north of us, and in all honesty, somewhere behind us.

"What's your call, John?" Sarah asked.

I pulled over to look at the map. Even though we were the only ones on the road, I didn't need to off road it right now.

"I think our best bet is to stay where we are, and cross the bridge at Hennepin. I've thought about these guys and going through water, and nothing we've seen so far tells me they like water anymore than the regular Z's," I said.

"What about the wet zombie's we saw?" Sarah asked.

"I forgot about the rain that hit us. Chances are that they just got caught in a storm, and why would they seek shelter like we would?" I asked.

The radio popped to life. "You planning on moving soon?" Charlie's voice came over the speaker.

I picked up the transmitter. "Hang on. Trying to figure where to go from here. Two minutes."

"Oh. Take your time. Charlie out."

"The waterways should steer them south, whether they're trying or not. Freeman's got the northern end sealed up, it looks like, and there's nothing but dead towns along the I-80 corridor. Princeton's dead, and if Freeman had half a brain…hold on." I grabbed the transmitter. "Tommy, can you raise any army people?"

"Not really. We're too small and there's too many hills with the river valley to get a good signal., Tommy replied, "Why?"

"Never mind, just had an idea," I said. "Out." I looked at Sarah. "If we could get him to deploy along 180, then he'd have the advantage of cover and give the zombies a serious fight."

Sarah looked at it. "Yeah, and send them all south, which, if they stayed on their course to the east, would put them in our backyard. Maybe not."

I looked again. Damn, she was right. Thank God, we couldn't reach Freeman. "All right. Let's get moving and get ourselves on the right side of the river. With luck, we could be home this evening."

Sarah squeezed my hand. "Magic words, Mr. Talon. Make it happen."

CHAPTER 23

I drove as quickly as I could, dodging the worst of the potholes and cracks, slowing for the other ones. Road maintenance was the lowest of priorities in the post-Upheaval world, and it was up to the communities to do it themselves. The roads outside of the communities suffered the most, with only I-80 being the most regularly maintained. It just meant that a trip that should have taken ten minutes was now a half an hour or more. In some parts of the country, it was literally faster to walk.

We reached Route 29, and I gratefully pointed the truck north. A half mile later, we were on I-180, grinning like kids who start to see the signs for the amusement park they have been travelling forever to get to.

One mile later and I was out of the truck, staring in disbelief at the ruined bridge in front of me. Sarah was by my side, and the rest of the crew was staring as well.

A barge was half-sunk in the river, after colliding with the center support. The impact had cracked the bridge, and subsequent freezes and thaws had widened the cracks, allowing for great chunks of the bridge to fall into the river below. At most, there was about two feet of bridge left to cross to get to the undamaged side and across the water. Twisted metal hung down, supporting hunks of concrete, making the bridge look like it had been bombed. The barge was rusted and decayed, telling me this accident had happened years ago, back when people were using whatever they could to get to some kind of safety. The irony was they could have just stayed on the barge in the middle of the city and been perfectly safe.

"Are you kidding me?" Duncan asked, summing up what all of us felt.

I sighed. "Let's find a way around. Hopefully there's another bridge close by."

We climbed back into our vehicles and I turned south. Sarah and I didn't say much, but we were feeling the same thing. This was just a delay we didn't need or want.

Seven miles south and another half an hour later, we were looking at the afternoon sun shining on the small town of Henry. Henry was a river town that managed to survive the Upheaval, by diverting part of the river to form a barrier around the three defenseless sides of the community. We stopped only briefly to tell the people there about the possible threat, and they responded by posting a watch on the town's water tower. If anything came within ten miles, they'd know right away.

We drove through the rest of Henry, and I had to admit, it was a nice town. People had gardens they were tending, there were a lot of children running around, and for the most part, people seemed to have moved on from the tragedy of the earlier years. It was a good thing to see, after all of the dead towns we had been to over the course of the last week.

As nice as Henry was, the nicest part was the lovely, intact, unbroken bridge that crossed the Illinois River. I nearly had tears in my eyes as I crossed the water to the other side. We were sixteen miles from home, as the crow flew, and I almost became nostalgic for a horse.

I took us east on 18, then turned north on 89. I couldn't use I-39, since that was a backed up disaster of cars and zombies. Once the wars were over, I had decided to open only one road south, and I-39 wasn't it. The only thing we had done was seal the exits so the zombies that did free themselves from the cars had nowhere to go, and the elements would take care of them.

As we reached the intersection of 71 and 89, Tommy called over on the radio.

"John? We might want to look at Grainville." Tommy sounded disturbed.

Shit. Nothing was going well. "Why?" I hoped it was a good reason and not some weird farm festival.

"I'm getting a looped distress signal."

That wasn't a good sign. Could the little zombies have beaten us here? "Is it on regular channels?"

"The military one."

Oh, hell. "All right. Tell everyone to gear up, this could be bad." I put the receiver down and looked over at Sarah just as she shook her head.

"It's not fair. What did we do so wrong?" she asked as she checked her magazines.

I thought for a moment. "I think it was when we told Dot we'd take this stupid mission. Lesson learned."

I turned left onto 71 and could see the outskirts of Grainville immediately. There was a lot of smoke rising in the sky, and from where we were, we could see at least two houses on fire. I turned up Elm Street to get into the town proper, and it was bad from the beginning. Two torn bodies were draped over each other inside a car; the door was flung open and covered in blood.

I turned west on Main Street, and there were more bodies. Some were lying flat on their face; others were crouched in little balls in corners of buildings. Pools of blood decorated their places of death.

The bodies grew in number as we went further west. There were older and younger dead here, as well as a number of dead zombie kids. A small park in the center of town looked like it might have been used as a place of a last stand. Dozens of bodies covered a small white gazebo.

The sight of that gazebo brought a lot of memories flooding back, and none of them was too pleasant. I just kept shaking my head as we moved slowly through the carnage.

West Main Street ended at Division Street, and I turned north to see if there was any chance of survivors. At the turn, I moved the truck back the way I had come and headed south. At the intersection of Division and South Street, I thought I saw a military truck, so I headed back east. Sarah had said nothing this whole time, just shaking her head at the mess of everything.

At the end of the road, there were three military trucks, and a lot of empty brass lying on the ground. We had run out of road, so I got out of the truck and slowly approached the vehicle. Charlie and Tommy were out and circling wide, while Duncan kept a watch on our backs. Sarah and Rebecca walked carefully to the south, looking for anyone who might have survived.

The truck cab was clean, but I noticed the radio had an odd yellow light that was flashing in a regular pattern. I flicked it off, wondering if I had cancelled the distress call.

"Over here!" Charlie called. He had gone down the small embankment, and through the bushes.

I made my way down and cursing as a sticker bush scratched my hand, joined Charlie on a small peninsula of land. A small creek made an oxbow here, and it was here we found the remains of fifty of Freeman's soldiers. They had retreated to this spot, and thought to defend it. It wasn't a bad place, but I could see where a problem could be. Behind the oxbow was a hill, and at the top of that hill was a railroad track. The kids could have easily stormed the position without a shot being fired.

They didn't get it for free, though. About a dozen zombie kids were lying about in various poses, and their snarling faces and vicious leers told me they weren't the children of the town.

We weren't alone, however. Two forms burst from the bushes and threw themselves at Charlie and me, little hands ready to grab and little mouths ready to bite.

Charlie was almost contemptuous as he backhanded the taller of the two with the hammer side of one of his 'hawks. It fell sideways, and before it could get set, he clobbered it with his other one.

The smaller one, a boy, ran at me with his face torn open. His teeth showed through his cheek, and his right eyebrow looked to have been torn off. He jumped at me, trying to get to my face and neck.

I wasn't about to give him the chance. I swung hard with my pick, connecting with the side of his head with the flat edge, stopping the attack cold. The body fell in a heap, and I realized I had swung hard enough to crack its neck.

I looked over at Charlie. "Took you two." I chided.

Charlie frowned. "The sun was in my eyes."

I looked around. "The sun isn't anywhere near your eyes!" I complained.

"Exactly," Charlie said, turning and walking away through the bushes.

I just shook my head and followed. We got back to the vehicles just as Tommy and Duncan came walking in, having walked a bit further south. They reported that there were a lot of dead people by the creek, and quite a few zombie kids.

"Looks like this place didn't just lie down and die," Tommy said.

"Well, it still doesn't look good," I said.

"You mean clean up?" Duncan asked. "We could do that quickly enough."

"No, I meant there doesn't seem to be any kids, outside of the ones that run with the zombies."

That got their attention. All of the kids from one or two towns was a significant force, and not to be taken lightly. If the force that hit Freeman just got bolstered by another hundred, we were looking at maybe three hundred zombie kids. And as far as we knew, they were headed straight for home.

"Let's get to putting them down for good. We don't have a lot of time," I said.

We got back in the truck and I sat on the tailgate with Charlie, while Tommy drove. Sarah and Rebecca were sweeping the town center for survivors. We hoped to find someone who had managed to shelter somewhere while the disaster played out.

Tommy drove slowly, and we took turns getting out and spiking the heads of the people that were down. It was grisly work, no matter how you looked at it, and we were just past Turner Street when we saw the bodies were starting to stir.

Charlie thumped on the tailgate. "Better get past this and into a clearer area!" He yelled at Tommy, moving back. I slid back onto the bed of the truck and pulled the tailgate closed.

CHAPTER 24

A dead hand reached up just as I closed it, and as we drove away, the owner of the hand slowly got to his feet. If you had to face a zombie that was standing, this was the best time. They were just getting their bearings and just figuring out how to walk. You had about ten seconds to decide what you were going to do with them.

Fortunately, we had been here before. I took the right side and Charlie took the left. Bracing ourselves in the space between the wheel well and the tailgate, we took swings at zombie heads as we drove past. Tommy kept us to about five miles an hour, and swerved like a lunatic to try and get them all. We had both nearly fallen out twice as Tommy circled to get one that we couldn't reach. The best part was that if Tommy misjudged, he took it out anyway, since the bumper killed a zombie just as quickly as a pickaxe or a tomahawk. The only danger was sometimes a zombie got the timing right and landed on the edge of the truck bed just in front of us. The momentum of the truck slid them right at you quickly, and you could choose to duck and let them pass, or be damn quick on the kill.

I usually let them pass. We always came back for them anyway. Charlie angled a 'hawk so they bumped upright, and he took them out as they fell back. It was more efficient than my method, but it didn't matter.

Tommy turned down the main business road, and we were confronted with a near wall of zombies. From Putnam County Public Library to Grainville Bancshares, there had to be at least seventy newly pressed zombies lurching around and leaving several kinds of nasty all over the landscape.

Charlie looked over at me. "Your call."

I thought for a second. "Well, we do have that extra ammo from Freeman's boys. Let's pull them out of there." I thumped on the roof. "Back up, slowly, and hit the horn a few times."

"Got it." Came the answer through the back window of the truck.

The truck backed up slowly, honking loudly to get the attention of the zombies. I laid over the cab roof, with Charlie doing the same next to me. He had a bipod on his rifle; I was going to have to use my elbows.

"I got the left of the center line, chief," Charlie said, looking through his scope and firing. His shot took out the lead zombie and the one right behind it.

"Nice. I'm on it," I said, lining up and taking a shot which took out a woman in her mid fifties.

We fired for a good ten minutes, with Tommy backing up slowly the whole time. We dropped them in doorways, in the street, and in the ditches. By the time we reached Yespen Chiropractic Health Center, we had taken the horde apart.

I was refilling a magazine when Tommy stuck his arm out the rear window. He was holding the microphone for the CB and it sounded like someone had poked a cat with a sharp stick and was letting it vent on the other end.

"Hello?" I said.

Duncan's voice came through loud and clear. "What's the third rule of firearm safety?"

What the hell? "I don't have time for...Oh, shit." I looked down the street, and sure enough, the van was there. "Anyone hurt?" I asked, concerned.

Duncan replied. "Just the front tires. I figure you two morons put three rounds apiece in them.

Damn. I looked over at Charlie and his shoulders slumped. "Well, we'll be there shortly, Talon out."

"Shit, damn, and double shit. This is our fault," I said.

"Let's fix it first, and then blame Duncan later," Charlie said.

I couldn't argue with that, so we headed back down the street. At the other end, the van sported eleven new vents, courtesy of yours truly. I opened the door to Sarah kicking me in the chest and knocking me over. Charlie laughed only once, and then Rebecca kicked him behind the knees and he dropped quicker than I did. From the ground, we looked at our spouses.

"Would it help to say I was sorry?" I asked, reaching for a hand up.

"If you ever...So help me, I'll...Of all the irresponsible...Oooo!" Sarah slapped my hand away and stalked off, presumably to find something zombie like so she could vent her frustrations properly. I was just grateful she hadn't decided to do it on me.

Tommy helped me to my feet, and I helped Charlie up after I had removed Rebecca from standing on his chest. She took a swing at me, but missed by a mile. Charlie watched her stalk off after Sarah.

"Well, you know what they say. Any encounter with the opposite sex you walk away from..." Charlie said.

I laughed. "All too true. Let's get the stuff into the truck, and we'll put it in the big truck to take back home."

We unpacked the van, and it took a heck of a lot longer than I thought it would. The sun was in its deep setting stage, with streaks of pink and red arcing across the sky as the rays found clouds we couldn't see. The darkening sky of the east reached out with purple tendrils to try and push the sun past the horizon.

I was tempted to spend the night out here, but I couldn't do it anymore, and I couldn't do it to Sarah.

CHAPTER 25

We packed up and moved out, leaving a dead town behind. There was nothing to be done for it, so we moved on. I was more concerned about my family, and I could see that Sarah was, too.

We drove as quickly as we could, skirting Oglesby and staying on 71. That took us to our own back yard and in an hour, just as night lay full claim to the sky. We drove through familiar territory, and were able to make decent time thanks to the fact that the country roads were deserted.

I took us down the long driveway to Starved Rock Lodge, and Sarah was practically giddy. I was excited as well, looking forward to sleeping in my own bed and seeing my sons again. We had been gone for too long, and I knew we hadn't finished the job. But we did what we needed to do, and would let this night just be for us.

At the front entrance, I parked and got out, followed closely by the rest of the crew. We were tired, worn out, and smelled like death, but we were home. By all that's holy, we were home.

Duncan threw the first cup of cold water on the scene. "Why are the lights off?"

I looked around. Sure enough, it was dark. We normally kept a couple on, just in case someone stopped by. We didn't get many visitors, but enough to be polite with the lights.

"Don't know. Strange," I said. "Let's do a quick check, before we go in."

Charlie, Duncan, Tommy and I did a quick sweep of the lodge. All of our defenses were in place, and nothing had been broken. For all intents and purposes, the place was fine.

I stepped to the door, drawing my pistol. "Just in case," I said to several quizzical looks.

I unlocked the door, including the two deadbolts. Once inside, the darkness was deep, and many corners were hidden in shadows. Nothing seemed out of sorts, but it just wasn't right.

I motioned to Tommy and Duncan to go check upstairs, while the rest of us checked out the main lodge area and the balcony. In the main hall, I flicked the switch and bathed us in bright light.

"Well, that works," I said, walking over to the balcony.

"I don't see anything amiss out there," Charlie said.

"Well, what the hell?" I said. "Where's Janna and Angela?"

Duncan came striding into the hall, with his wife and child right behind him. Tommy came in holding Angela's hand, and she held her child as well. Angela gave Sarah and Rebecca a quick hug, and then turned to me.

"The little zombies were here, John. They couldn't get in, so they left. We heard firing coming from your brother's place." Angela's voice was full of concern.

My blood went cold. "Where's Jake and Aaron?" I asked quickly.

"They're still over there."

Oh, sweet Jesus. No.

CHAPTER 26

"John, you can't run out there! The zombies are still in the woods!"

"John, no! Stop!"

"Charlie, stop him! Wait, where are you going? *Charlie*!"

I fairly flew through the woods, running as hard as I could for my brother's lodge. I only had my sidearm, my knife, and my trench hawk, but I didn't care. Absolutely nothing was going to stop me from getting to my sons. If a zombie kid showed up, he'd be put through a tree, no questions asked.

Charlie ran alongside me, both hands filled with his weapons. He didn't speak, and we didn't have to. There was no need to discuss plans or strategies. We were just going to go in and kill anything that wasn't related to him or me.

We crested the ridge that overlooked my brother's lodge, and slid downhill partway. We had to go a little slower, since the trails were rougher here, but we still made better time than we would have had we taken the trucks. The roads weren't direct out here, and we covered the ground in little under two minutes.

We ran up to the front entrance, and already things didn't look good. There was about fifteen zombie kids scattered around the parking lot, each one with a shot to the head. That was probably Nicole's shooting. Mike wasn't the best with a rifle, but he might have made the shots with a handgun. Charlie looked one over and made a hand signal that told me they had been killed by a rifle.

I moved along the wall of the building, and the broken windows didn't tell me good news. The zombies had swarmed this place, and they didn't bother to knock. One of the heavy, wooden front doors was open, and there were about seven small corpses piled on top of each other. These had smaller wounds, done by a handgun.

Charlie and I crossed the dead pile and entered the building. The lights were still on, which was a good thing for us. We wouldn't have to hunt in the dark. Charlie went over to the counter, and looked around while I looked over by the hallway leading towards the bank of rooms on the west side.

"Couple of empty magazines here, about twenty spent cases, 9mm." Charlie said.

"Any blood?" I asked, looking out over the water park.

"Not yet."

Hoping for a miracle, I took the stairs to the balcony. At the top, I found more spent shells, and several more zombie kids. Their peaceful expressions seemed to mock me as I hunted for my own children. I ran down the west hall, calling out for anyone.

"Mike! Nicole! Jake! Anyone? It's John! Somebody answer me!" I pounded on the doors as I went past, and I could hear Charlie doing the same below me. The silence was deafening and my heart was pounding. *Where were my children?*

Moving back to the main lobby, I started down the east wing and stopped cold. On the wall were small drops of blood. The spray pattern looked like someone had been injured and flung the blood away from themselves. I touched the blood drops and my finger came away sticky. This blood was recent, no more than an hour old.

"Mike! It's John! Where the hell are you? Where's my sons?" I yelled, moving down the hall. I kept my Springfield out, ready to blast away any leftover zombie kids. But the halls were as silent as the grave, filling me with dread.

At the end of the hall, there was another pile of zombies at the top of the stairs. I looked down and saw several more, lying on the steps, each one shot in the head. This wasn't making any sense. Mike knew enough to build retreats into his plans, why the hell would he make a stand here.

"John?" Charlie's voice came up the stairs, startling me.

"Find something?" I asked, hopeful and scared at the same time.

"Not yet, the downstairs is clear on this side of the hotel," Charlie said. He was as stressed as I was. His daughter was here somewhere, too.

"I'm coming down," I said.

I ran back to the main stairwell in the lobby and fairly jumped down to the main level. We looked around, and I began to wonder if maybe they had gotten out and were holed up in one of the cabins outside. That would have been a tactical mistake, but who knows. I was wishing at this point that I had paid more attention to how my brother had set up his defenses in case of an attack.

On the opposite side of the reservation counter, a hallway led along the length of the building. I looked at it and motioned to it with my trench hawk.

"Did you check that hallway?" I asked Charlie, who was standing by the big bay windows that looked out over the water park.

Charlie turned around. "Didn't see that one. I think we want to check the park."

"What? Why?" I asked, coming over to the window.

"I can't see it clearly, but there's something not right in there. I wish these windows were cleaner," Charlie said.

I thought for a second. I was torn between checking the hallway and checking the water park. I opted for the hallway, since whatever happened here was done, and two more minutes wouldn't matter anyway. I didn't say that to Charlie, but I started to get that sinking feeling in my gut. If we didn't find our kids here, we weren't going to. They would be gone, recruited into the army of the enemy, and there was nothing left for us to save.

CHAPTER 27

I walked over to the hall and started down it. There was a lot of violence in this area. Zombie kids and parts of them were all over the place, some still moving. We found three of them that had been shot in the neck, their spines broken. They still blinked and snapped their teeth, but that ended when we reached them.

Further down the hall, the carnage got worse. There were kids with their heads blown apart, and others that didn't have heads at all. These were piled on top of each other, and we had to be careful when we pulled them out of the way that they didn't try and bite one of us.

I looked at Charlie and we both sighed. "Looks like a last stand, doesn't it?" I said.

Charlie looked up sharply. "Don't say that! It's not over until we see it for ourselves."

I looked at Charlie and his eyes were wider than normal. He was on the brink, and whatever we found at the end of this hallway, would be either relief or rage.

We passed a small desk and moved into the back area, which was a large meeting room. Chairs were all over the place, and there were more zombie dead back here. The path of the dead zombies led to a small stage at the back, and there were several up on the stage.

My brother was on the stage as well. He was seated on a chair, and I could tell he was dead. His head hung down and off to one side. A casual glance could cause someone to mistake him for sleeping, but the numerous wounds in his arms and legs would change that assessment. He had been bitten several times, and had lost a considerable amount of blood. Looking around, I could see that he had fought until the very end, and then denied the zombies their final victory by putting his last bullet in his own head.

I knelt down by my brother. "Oh, Mike. I'm so sorry." I took his guns and tucked them in my belt, both his beloved Beretta 92 and his Smith 460. That gun caused so much devastation, but couldn't be reloaded fast enough to stop them all. I couldn't do anything for a long time but sit by my brother and let the tears flow. We'd been through so much, and he had survived so much. It wasn't fair that he went out like this, not fair at all. He'd managed to get his family out of the worst of the Upheaval, survive a trip downriver, keep them alive until I could find him, then start to rebuild his life with his family.

Now he was dead. I had never felt such a deep loss, not since I lost Ellie. I had no hope of finding my sons now. I felt they were gone too, and that loss was almost too much.

"I'm so sorry," I said again. "I shouldn't have left you. You weren't ready. I'm so sorry." I couldn't shake the feeling that my kids were gone, and a black pit opened beneath me, pulling my heart in.

I don't know how long I sat there, but I was shaken out of my misery by Charlie suddenly grabbing my brother and shaking his dead form.

"Where's my daughter? Goddamn you, *where's my daughter?*" Charlie shouted into Mike's blank face. Charlie lifted Mike's body off the chair and held him up, shaking him and shouting.

"Charlie! What the hell are you doing?" I pulled Mike's body away from Charlie and laid it down on the stage. I arranged it as best I could, and when I turned back to Charlie, I nearly pulled my gun at the look on his face.

Charlie ignored me, lunging towards Mike's body again, so lost in his emotions that he didn't comprehend Mike was dead and couldn't give him any answers. *"Where is she?"* He shouted again, his hands gripping his tomahawks so tightly that his knuckles nearly glowed white in the gloom.

I got in his way and pushed back, my grief slowed by the anger that was rising at Charlie's behavior.

Charlie spread his arms wide, and I wrapped him up, lifting him off his feet and propelling him backwards. I tripped over a small body and we went down in a tangle of arms and legs. I got to my feet first and placed myself between Mike and Charlie.

Charlie got to his feet, and his head slumped down. His arms hung loosely at his sides, and I doubted he even realized he was holding his weapons. I put a hand out to his shoulder, and he suddenly fell to his knees.

"I can't..." Charlie whispered. "I'm not strong enough..."

I went to one knee, and put my arms around Charlie's head. His chest heaved with emotion and he shook with sobs.

"I can't lose another daughter, John," Charlie cried. "I'm not strong enough to do it again."

I had nothing to say, understanding the hollowness of his heart right now. I could do nothing but hold my friend and pray we might find a miracle.

After a few minutes, Charlie shook me off, and got to his feet. His eyes were red and he sniffed a lot, but I figured he was placing his grief in a place that only he could access, and only by himself.

We didn't say a word, we just went over to my brother and picked him up. I could have carried him by myself, but I knew Charlie had to help.

At the end of the hall, we took a break, placing Mike's body in the lobby. Charlie walked over to the big bay windows that looked out over the water park and stared for a long time. I stood next to him, not knowing what to say, not trusting myself to say anything. All I could see in my mind was the faces of my boys, and every memory caused another pang of grief to spike through my heart.

CHAPTER 28

Suddenly Charlie stiffened. "I saw movement."

I snapped out of my despair, hope suddenly soaring. "Where?" I scanned the park desperately, searching for anything.

"Way in the back, up on a platform," Charlie said, turning away to look for an entrance to the park.

I was right on his heels, and we raced through a small arcade on the ground floor, past a bar, through a snack shop, and past a locker room. We burst out onto the water park, nearly slipping into a small wading pool designed for little kids.

The park was huge, and had a lot of brightly colored tubes going all over the place. There was a large pool over to our right, some fake rocks and a bridge going over to a huge Jacuzzi.

Charlie ran over to another bridge which crossed a lazy river. On the other side was an island with a fake bamboo fortress which sported a huge cauldron of water, which spilled over every once in a while. Two small water slides arced around the structure, ending together on the left side of the island.

"Here!" I called leaping over another bridge. This one led us to the stairs at the back of the water park. These stairs led upwards to the larger water slides, one was painted red and the other a deep green. I was pounding up the stairs, with Charlie right behind me. As I reached the last landing before the top, I stopped. The stairs in front of me were tilted downward, balanced on a bar that allowed for a section of the steps to spin in a circle unless they were secured by a wooden dowel, which was hanging by a rope.

"Hold this end," I said, stepping onto the stairs. The far end swung towards me, but stopped as Charlie secured the end with his hands and feet. I moved cautiously but quickly, grabbing the peg and sliding it into a slot under the stairs. As soon as I did that, Charlie and I were up the last flight, not bothering to conceal our steps.

As we rounded the corner, we both hit the floor as a shot screamed past our heads. I felt the passage of the bullet as it creased the air near my face, and I slid to a stop at the doorway.

"Nicole! It's John and Charlie!" I shouted, praying as I had never prayed before.

"Dad!" Jake shouted.

"Daddy!" Julia shouted.

"Daddy!" Aaron shouted.

I had never heard sounds so wonderful in my life. My heart suddenly flew open, and the tears flowed again as my children ran and toddled over. I pulled them both off the ground, holding one in each arm, trying to hug and kiss each face at the same time.

Charlie was standing, holding his beloved daughter off the ground, burying his face in her shoulder and neck. He said nothing, he just held her as he sobbed in relief.

"John? Did you see Mike? Is he okay?" Nicole was standing off to the side, holding her children. Her eyes were red and wet, and she stared at me with an intensity I knew all too well.

I put my children down, and walked slowly over to Nicole. I didn't have to say anything, she could read it on my face, and see it in the weapons on my belt.

"He died saving all of you," I said finally. No greater epitaph could exist for a man who loved his family.

"Oh, Mike. Oh, no." Nicole sat heavily, still holding her children. She cried for a long time, and her children, when they understood what their mother was crying about, joined her in her sorrow.

We left the water park in silence, and I sent Charlie on ahead with Nicole over to the other lodge. They left through a side door, and walked around the parking lot. Charlie was careful not to let the children see their dead father and uncle.

I carried Mike all the way back to Starved Rock, ignoring the pain in my legs and arms. My brother died for my sons, and I sure as hell wasn't going to put him down now. All the way, I talked to him, telling him about what I was going to teach his children, and how he wouldn't have to worry about anyone looking after them. I told him to tell Mom and Dad about Jake and Aaron, and that I'd see them in due time. I wrapped him up in a blanket, and placed him in an unused room in the lodge.

CHAPTER 29

In the morning, I took a large pickaxe and shovel, and with Charlie by my side, we hiked out to the Eagle's Nest overlook, and spent the morning carving out a grave in the limestone.

I lay my brother to rest that afternoon, and with everyone gathered, spoke about my brother. I talked about how we grew up, how we drove our parents crazy, and how we competed in a lot of things. I spoke of his love for family, and how that love caused him to lay down his life to protect those he cared about. Finally, I talked about how I was proud to know him, and honored to call him my brother.

Everyone else spoke briefly about Mike, telling small stories, relating bits of information to weave into a life narrative. When we were done, everyone save Charlie and myself went back to the lodge. We filled the grave, and Charlie placed a small stone marker with the name Mike Talon carved into it.

Two days later, Nicole left with the children. She wanted nothing to do with the wilderness, or the place that had claimed her husband's life. Taking a spare boat, she barely glanced goodbye at us as she went upriver. I didn't try and stop her, I understood what she was doing. There was nothing here for her, and the thing that held her here was gone.

For the next three days, the phone rang, people calling us about attacks and little zombies. I had given my report to Dot, and I was finished. They had an army, they had veterans, and I wasn't needed.

That didn't stop Dot from trying. Every day she called about a new attack, and how a huge horde of little zombies was making its way across the countryside, wiping out towns and getting larger with zombies kids. The last report had the horde making its way through Joslyn, working its way up the river. Dot told us that Freeman had quit, and sent his army home, leaving the capital defenseless.

I was unmoved. This expedition had cost me my brother, and nearly cost me my sons. I had done my part and wanted nothing more than to be left alone. Sarah didn't press me on it, and the rest of the crew felt the same way I did. We had fought, bled and sacrificed, and it was time for us to be left alone.

Three days after Nicole had left, Sarah found me practicing with my hawk and a small sword Duncan had given me. It was a single edged blade about two and a half feet in length, and had a metal basket that covered the hand that held it. It was unsophisticated, designed to hack and stab. It suited my style perfectly.

"John?" Sarah asked.

"What's up?"

"Charlie told me to tell you there's a man standing by your brother's grave."

That was odd. Mike didn't really have any friends, and none that would make a trip from the capital just to visit his grave.

I belted on my pistol, and tucked my trench hawk in place. "Anything else?"

Sarah nodded. "Charlie said the man moved well, like he knew how to fight."

I grunted in surprise. That was high praise from Charlie, who was the best fighter I knew. "All right, I'll go check it out. Maybe it's an old friend from before that ran into Nicole."

I walked out onto the patio, and made my way over to the stairs that led to the river valley floor. I had a decent hike ahead of me, and wasn't really looking forward to it. I was in a bit of a funk these days, and the damn phone ringing all the time didn't help. I felt a bit guilty about not running to the rescue of the capital, but I guessed I was mad at the way things turned out. I was mad that Dot never once said she was sorry for Mike getting killed.

The hike up to the Eagle's Nest took me about a half hour, and I could see the man standing up there as I worked my way up the western side. Thankfully, there were stairs up to this point, and in my current mood, I would have been seriously put out if I had had to climb up here.

At the top, I was surprised as usual by the beauty of the region. The morning sun glanced off the river bend, sending bright lancets of light over the trees and cliffs. The flashing colors of the autumn leaves contrasted nicely with the pale blue of the sky. Retreating clouds gave way to the sun, showing their pinkish backsides as they fled over the horizon.

The man standing at my brother's grave was a bit shorter than I was, though just as broad. His shoulders were slightly stooped, though from age or grief I couldn't tell yet. His head was slightly bent, and from my angle, I could see a hand covering a bearded mouth.

His head turned slightly at my approach, and I stopped about fifteen feet back. I was slightly annoyed at the intrusion at my brother's grave, but if this were a friend, I would understand.

"Name's John Talon," I said as a way of greeting. "Did you know my brother?"

The man turned his head slightly at the sound of my name, and I could see a bit more of his face. The eye I could see looked tired, lined with both grief and joy. The hand that covered his mouth was scarred, but looked strong, as if it had known a lifetime of good, hard work. His longish hair was mostly grey, but there were dark areas as well.

His clothing was neat and clean, and there was nothing of the vagabond about this man. His pack, resting at his feet, was of a military type, with dozens of pockets and places to store needed items.

At his belt was a single pistol, a 1911 style like mine, and a worn, leather-handled knife. Three loaded magazines rested next to the knife.

"I knew him. I knew him for a long time." The man's voice was slightly raspy, and somewhat choked up. I tried to place the man as a family friend, but was coming up blank. I was very curious as to who this man was.

"How did he die?" The next question came as a whisper. "Was it the sickness?"

"No," I said. "He was watching my sons and his family while I was away. His home was attacked. He died saving his family and mine." I began to get a little choked up myself, thinking about that night when I thought I lost everything.

The man shook a little, and I realized he was trying to hold back sobs. I didn't know what else to say, so I just let him have his moment.

After a few minutes, the man composed himself. "So he died well. Good." The man placed a hand on the marker and said. "God speed, boy."

The man straightened himself up, and shook his head, probably trying to get his emotions in check. I was extremely curious about the identity of this man, and waited for him to gather his pack and get himself situated.

The man stood for a long time, staring out over the river. I didn't know what to say other than, "How did you know my brother?"

The man turned and faced me. His eyes were red and his cheeks were stained with tears. But his bearing was straight, and as I looked, I thought I had seen this man before. Something about him was extremely familiar, and my subconscious was screaming his name at me.

The man gave a half smile. "I knew him the same way I know you."

I couldn't stop the sudden flow of tears, or the way my shoulders sagged at the man standing in front of me. I don't know how I managed to keep from falling to my knees. All I could do was hold out a hand and say the first thing I could think of.

"Hey, Dad."

CHAPTER 30

My father sat at the big table, surrounded by the rest of the extended family. I sat next to him, and held Aaron in my lap. As he spoke, he kept reaching out and touching Aaron's hand, almost as if he couldn't believe he had another grandson. Jake was sitting in his grandfather's lap, snuggled in like only little boys can do. My dad's arm was wrapped protectively around Jake, and every now and then, he would pat his first grandson on the side, keeping him safe. We had spent a good deal of time on introductions, and Dad was very kind to Sarah, thanking her for keeping me sane and giving him another grandson. When Dad met Charlie, he shook hands like he'd known him all his life, and told Charlie he was honored to meet such a famous zombie killer. Charlie nearly blushed.

"Well, I guess I could start at the beginning," my dad said. "When we started hearing rumors of things going south in the big cities, I started to get my things together. I had friends in the police force in Baltimore, and they let me know how bad things really were. The media, the ones that most people watch, I figure they could take the blame for a lot of what happened. People knew the truth a long time before the event, and they didn't tell anyone. Imagine what we could have avoided had they told us in the beginning what we were facing. Makes me sick." Dad stopped for a minute to take a drink and then continued.

"I figured we could have made it work in Virginia, the house was pretty isolated and we had good water nearby with a well-stocked forest in the back yard. My neighbor, Bill, was a Navy man; he and I spent a good deal of time going over what we would do and how we would survive. Instead of building fortresses, we'd figure on stealth. Let the dead walk by and leave us alone.

"That was the plan. But when your mom got sick, well, the plan went with her. I buried her with my own hands; after I had to make sure she stayed dead."

I thought for a second, and then asked. "Did you have to…?" I didn't complete the sentence, but I didn't need to.

Dad looked at me with sympathy. "No, son. I didn't wait for her to wake up. I put a .22 into her head, 'cause I knew she'd be getting up and coming after me. She was dead, and I wasn't hurting her." Dad looked down. "Still one of the hardest things I ever done."

"Anyway," he continued. "I buried your mom and wrote those letters for you and Mike. I couldn't stay in that house, there were too many memories, so I packed up and left. I kept to the woods, living in the wilds, working my way down the Appalachian Trail. That was some deep country, let me tell you, and there were some strange folk out there, but they left me alone. I did have to shoot one man for trying to stick a knife in me, but that was it."

Charlie grunted and Dad smiled at him. "Yeah, I can take care of myself, young fella. Don't you worry about this old Marine."

Charlie grinned. "Wasn't worried about you, just anyone you might take a disliking to."

Dad laughed. "So I was heading south, and I found myself wandering from community to community, showing people how to defend themselves and teaching the basics of hand to hand combat to others. I met some real good people out there, and some real idiots. They're probably all dead, since the waves from the cities pretty much wiped out anyone living, as you all figured out."

Dad paused again, and took another drink. He held Aaron's hand again, and gave Jake a hug. "When I hit Georgia, I decided to just keep going south. I figured the Keys would be a good place to get away and hold up for a while, so I headed that way. Along the way, I heard about a big crowd of people who decided to make Disneyworld their little fortress. Don't know what happened to them, but I wished them luck."

Tommy spoke up. "They didn't make it. Duncan and I were there a few years back. By the look of things, they tore themselves apart from within, without help from the Z's."

Dad absorbed this information with a simple, "Huh." He continued his narrative. "Well, then, I moved south, avoiding people and zombies. Seemed like there were more of the latter and less of the former every day. I made it to the Keys three days before they blew the bridge. That was a sorry sight, but it had to be done. Once there, I found myself a small apartment, and we got down to trying to survive. We had fish to eat, and the near daily rain kept us in fresh water. Fruit was all over, although I doubt I'll ever eat another orange as long as I live. We made it work. We had simple rules and everyone just tried to get through the day. Every once in a while, a boat would come by, and we'd keep an eye on them for a while, then either take them in or tell them to leave."

"What if they wouldn't go?" Duncan asked, leaning forward like a kid getting a scary story at bedtime.

"We changed their minds. I was in the security detail, and between me and a half dozen retired Army men, thirteen fresh Marines, and a quartet of Air Force mechanics, we made it work. If they didn't want to go, we persuaded them otherwise. The whole time I was there, we only had six encounters that involved shooting."

Dad paused again and then looked straight at me. "It was about three years in when I began to hear your name. Travelers from the north talked about a group that was putting the country back together, and there was a man leading the charge. I nearly had a heart attack when I found out it was you."

I smiled. "Just did what I had to do."

Sarah shook her head and leaned back into me as I wrapped an arm around her. Everyone else just grinned.

"I have to tell you son, I was damned proud to hear what you had done. You dug in and found out what I knew you had in you all along. These days, you mention your name and people remember you with respect and admiration."

I shook my head. "Not so much these days, I'll bet."

Dad looked at me again. "We'll see. Anyway, I nearly dropped into the ocean when I heard you were in the Keys. I was with a group looking for a band of pirates off the coast, and I made it back in time to see you sail away."

That was it! I knew I had seen him in Florida. "I remember. You were watching me as we sailed away. I thought I knew you then, but I wasn't sure."

"That was me. After that, I couldn't stay there. I began preparing to head north, but things always came up and I didn't get to leave for a few years. But then I heard about your war, and knew I had to get back to you before you went off and got yourself killed," Dad said.

I looked down. "No, I tend to get other people killed. It's a curse. Nate died on the trip to DC, Mike died when I went out to Iowa. I can't tell you how many followed me out west, and how many didn't come back."

"Not your fault, John. You never forced anyone to do anything. They knew the risks, and accepted them. I wish I had left earlier. I might have been able to be here and keep Mike alive."

We all were silent for a moment. Mike's death was a still an open wound, and I was about to say something when the phone rang. Everyone froze, and my dad looked at me.

"You going to answer it?" Dad asked.

"Nope. I've given enough. Someone else has to do it," I said.

Dad sighed and lifted Jake off his lap. He put him on the chair and walked over to the phone.

"John Talon, Sr."

CHAPTER 31

"John! Thank God, you answered the phone! Where the hell have you been? We've got outbreak reports from all over, and they seem to be converging on the capital! Wait, did you say, John Sr.?" We could hear the excited voice chattering on the other end.

"Go on."

"Holy crap, there's two of them. Could you tell him he needs to call the capital right away?"

"I'll tell him. 'Bye." Dad hung up the phone and walked behind me. He put a hand on my shoulder. "Let's head out to the patio."

I wasn't about to argue, so I disentangled myself from my family and followed my father outside. I had a good idea what he was going to say, or what he planned on saying, and I believed I could get the better of the argument.

Out on the porch, my dad looked around for a while, before drifting over to the side and staring out over the changing colors of the trees. I knew he was looking for Mike's grave, but he'd have to wait a bit before he could see it from here.

Dad turned and faced me. "You're wrong. Dead wrong."

"Wait, what?" I was taken off guard, which was a strange, uncomfortable feeling.

"Leaving these people to fend for themselves is the wrong thing to do. You may as well drive from town to town and kill them yourself," He said.

"They can take care of themselves. They don't need me." I said, defensively.

"More than ever, they need you," Dad said. "They have nearby, the one man who stood up and gave them a reason to go on, a reason not to put their last bullet through their own heads, and he's sitting this one out? You owe your brother more than that. You owe your sons more than that."

I looked him hard in the eyes. "You're damn right I owe them more. I owe them *me*. I've been running all over this country, from one fight to the next, and they've been left behind, wondering if their father is ever going to come back again, wondering if they are ever going to see *both* their parents again. Every time I wander off the reservation, someone close to me dies. First, it was Nate, and then it was Mike. Who's it going to be this time, Dad?"

Clearly, my father hadn't thought of this line of attack, and he was on the defense. "Well, I'd be staying with them this time, that's what would make this different."

"You ever see a horde of zombie kids up close?" I pressed my advantage. "They are fast and they are smart. They don't just come at you. They ambush and work around you. When you think you've got one pinned down, another comes from a direction you never thought of. In an instant, you can be overwhelmed. They aren't the slow, stupid ones we cut our teeth on. These will nail you to the wall and pick you apart in little bloody chunks."

Dad looked back at me. "That wasn't what I was talking about, anyway. You started this country back on track, and you owe it to your sons to make sure it stays that way. Right now, they can go just about anywhere and not have to worry too much about a zombie attack. They can set up homes of their own without having to make sure it can withstand a swarm. But if you let this go, if you let everything you ever fought for slide away, then you'll condemn them to living here, hoping for scraps to live on. Is that what you want?"

I hadn't thought about it that way, and the little seed of guilt that had been itching the back of my brain, suddenly sprouted and began to grow. I knew it was just a matter of time before I was saddled up and moving again.

I turned away and looked out over the forest. It truly was beautiful this time of year, and if you listened carefully, you could hear the falling water of the creek nearby that sustained us and kept us in good water.

I spoke to the river, flowing quietly away to the west. "I'm so tired," I whispered. I didn't expect any answer, but my father must have heard me, because he put a hand on my shoulder.

"I know, son. But like the great men of the old days, they did what was asked of them, because they knew it was the right thing to do. How they felt about it was irrelevant, and beneath consideration."

That kind of stung, but I knew what had to be done. "All right. Once more, into the breach." I turned around and to my surprise; my father had tears in his eyes.

"Just something in the air, don't mind me," Dad said, wiping his face with his sleeve.

I let it go, mostly because it was a little weird, and I had other things to do. I went back inside where everyone was still waiting. I looked at each of them in turn, and said to the group, "Change in plans."

Charlie looked at me out of the corner of his eyes. "Meaning?"

I looked back. "We're finishing this. All the way. I want all gear out and ready in an hour."

Duncan and Tommy jumped up, and raced each other to the supply room. Sarah and Rebecca gathered up the kids and hustled them out of the room. Janna and Angela followed, and I swore they were smiling.

I picked up the phone and dialed the capital. I had a direct line to the White House, and I knew Dot would take the call.

"White House, please state your business." The voice on the other end seemed strained, as if it had been receiving a lot of calls lately and was getting tired of being nice.

"I need to speak with Dot," I said.

"Madame President is busy at the moment, and will likely be busy in the near future. May I take a message?"

"It's John Talon."

There was a long pause, and then Dot's voice came through. "John? Good to hear from you. Listen, we've been getting a lot of reports of attacks by a large horde of child zombies and..."

I cut her off. "We're on our way. Fortify the capital and set up the communication links. I need the names of the last three towns hit, and I need to make a general call over the system. Can I have your permission to do that?"

Dot didn't hesitate. "Yes, and we will. We'll get you the names in a couple of minutes. Are you coming here?"

"If I have to, but we're going to run these bastards all the way. Call me soon." I hung up the phone and went over to a small room next to the bar. We had brought the long-range communication equipment up from its hiding place, and used it now to make a general call out. Every veteran of the Zombie Wars was required to have a radio in his or her house, turned on and tuned to one channel. If they received a message, they were required to act on that message. It was a modern version of the minutemen.

I turned on the equipment, which hummed satisfactorily. I flicked the switch to send and turned on the microphone.

"Attention. Attention. This is John Talon. Reserve battalions are hereby called up. All able reserves within the sound of my voice are recalled to duty effective immediately. You are to report to the capital within three days. Repeat, three days." I switched off the mic, and then turned off the equipment. We might get a hundred, we might get a thousand. Didn't really matter, because we were getting someone other than that poor excuse of an army.

The phone rang and Charlie picked it up. "Okay, okay, okay. Thanks. You heard the call? Good. We'll see you in a bit." He hung up the phone and pulled out a map. "South Ottowa had a sighting, and Grand Ridge was hit two days ago. If I were a betting man, I'd say the best place to hit them is at Marsielles Wildlife Area. Those woods are dense, and will slow them down."

"Good, we'll make for that area as soon as we can," I said.

"John, there's something else," Charlie said.

I didn't like the sound of this. "What?"

"The army is gone."

CHAPTER 32

"What? How? Where?" I nearly fell over.

"They got hit three days ago outside of Morris. There's a huge horde and they're headed right for Leport."

I thought for a second. "The river will slow them. Get on the horn and tell Dot to block all bridges that cross the river. Thank God, there's only four of them. Use cargo containers, anything, but get it done now. That's the only thing containing these little fuckers right now, is the damn river!" I yelled as I ran out to the garage to get out the big trucks. We weren't kidding around anymore. We were getting the big guns.

As I looked over our trucks, I realized we had better transportation at hand, and a better highway. I moved over to another garage, and opened it. Inside were three motorcycles. Two were BMW R1100's, and the other was a Honda CBR. I thought about it for a minute and the better and better it looked to me.

I fired up one of the BMW's and rode it down to the dock. Leaving it there, I ran, jogged, and walked my way back up the stairs and back to the garage. Fortunately, Duncan and Tommy were there, putting large duffle bags into the back of our biggest truck.

"Slight change in plans," I said as I started the second BMW.

Tommy eyed me doubtfully, and Duncan just looked like he normally does.

"Duncan, get on the rocket and follow me. Tommy, put together a duffle of shotguns and ammo," I said, pulling away.

"Shotguns? Why?" Tommy called after me, but I didn't have time to explain. Duncan and I rode down to the dock, and I left the second BMW there. I had Duncan give me a ride back to the garage where I met up with Tommy for the second time. Duncan rode off to the dock to carry out the instructions I had given him.

"Thanks, Tommy," I said, hefting a large duffle bag.

"What's the plan, John?" Tommy asked pointedly, flicking his head in the direction Duncan took.

"We're splitting up. Charlie, Duncan and I, are going to head off and kill the group that's south of 80, while you, Sarah and

Rebecca, head north of 80 and get to Leport as fast as you can. I don't know where the main horde is, but I'll be damned if I'm going to engage them wholesale when they might have a second group coming up to bite me in the ass," I said, putting the bag on like a backpack. The straps were going to cut into my arms, but it would only be for a short time.

Tommy flinched slightly, drawing a snarl on his face. "You think they're that sophisticated?"

I shook my head. "No, I think they're just pack animals now, and if you ask me why the hell they keep running east, even away from the main group, I haven't got an answer for you. But I *do* think they will eventually go off on their own, and when that thought goes through their diseased, dead brains, we may as well be in the second Upheaval."

Tommy mulled that one over for a second. "You know, in a weird kind of way, that makes sense and isn't as scary."

I slapped him on the shoulder. "Be afraid, my friend. It keeps us alive. Let's get going."

I went back into the lodge, mostly because it was the quickest way to the stairs and I knew Sarah would be waiting for me. I was slightly surprised to see my father there, but I could handle that.

"We're heading out upriver, and I need you and Rebecca to go with Tommy. You're going to go to Leport and set up defenses there," I said quickly, hoping to get out of a lengthy discussion.

Sarah looked at me with narrowed eyes. "Where are you going?"

"Charlie, Duncan and I, are taking a boat and getting over to the wilderness. The group that killed my brother is on their way there, and if we can get in there, we can hunt that group down and eliminate it as a threat. We'll meet you up in the capital." From my point of view, it sounded reasonable.

Sarah wasn't buying it. "What about Jake and Aaron?"

"My dad is here," I said. "I think he may have fired a gun or two in his life. I think Marines do that from time to time." I was getting impatient, and I tended to become a world-class smartass when that happened.

Dad spoke up, cutting Sarah off. "Sarah, it will be fine. Let John go, he needs to get that group. Get your stuff, and we'll talk."

I caught my father giving Sarah a wink, and my warning bells went off. Whatever was about to happen would be something I probably wouldn't like, but at the moment, there wasn't anything I could do about it.

"Do what you have to, but get moving. This horde isn't waiting for anyone," I said, as I went back out the door to the patio and the stairs. Charlie was waiting for me, and Rebecca was with him.

"Let's get moving. There's been a change in plan. Rebecca, you're going with Tommy and Sarah. We'll meet you at the capital," I said quickly.

Charlie raised an eyebrow. "Where are we going?" He asked.

"We're going hunting in the woods."

Charlie gave me a grin that was pure evil, and then kissed Rebecca goodbye. He picked up his own bag and headed off down the stairs. Just as he disappeared over the edge, Tommy rounded the corner. I waved him over to speak with him and Rebecca at the same time.

"Gather the veterans as they make their way to the capital. Set up as many retreating stations as you can, and keep that horde near the river. Do not let them get around you. Push them to the bridge at Leport as best as you can, then get to the capital. I'll see you there," I said.

"What if they don't cooperate?" Tommy asked. It was a legitimate question, and one that had serious repercussions.

I had nothing left but bravado. "Make them." With that, I turned and headed for the dock.

CHAPTER 33

Down by the boats, Duncan had managed to accomplish what I had asked of him. The three motorcycles were standing side by side on our pontoon boat, and the engine was idling, waiting for me to get my butt down there.

Charlie was lounging on the backbench, as if he had been there all morning, but I knew he had arrived a minute before I did.

I unwrapped the mooring lines and stepped aboard as Duncan eased up the throttle. The boat was low in the water, thanks to the weight of the cycles, but since this was a party boat, made once upon a time for a crowd of fat drunks, it handled it fine.

I put the duffle bag down and eased my shoulders before unzipping the bag. I pulled out the first shotgun and handed it to Charlie. The riverbanks slipped slowly by, and Duncan began to give the boat more throttle as he got used to the rhythm of the water and the weight of the boat.

I pulled the second shotgun out, and then the third, laying the two on the floor. I dumped out the rest of the duffle bag, which consisted of several boxes of buckshot, ranging in size from #4 to double ought. I gave a box to Charlie and he loaded the first gun up with five rounds of buck. Double ought buckshot contained nine balls roughly the same size as a .38 bullet, so some decent damage could be done if you worked the gun right.

I loaded the other two shotguns to capacity as well. The guns were Benelli M4's semi-auto shotguns we had picked up from an armory that hadn't been completely destroyed. When the Upheaval went bad, the regular army had received orders to destroy their armories, with the thought that civilians with superior firepower might not be so willing to obey the government if things got restored to normal. It was a monumentally bad decision, since more armed citizens could have stemmed the tide of zombies and contained the damage.

I loaded fifteen speed loaders, and Charlie loaded nine. Shotgun speed loaders were simple affairs. They were tubes with handles, and the first shell rested on the handle. You put rounds into the tube, and when it came time to reload, you put the end into the feed tube on the shotgun and shoved the handle forward. You could reload five rounds in a couple of seconds compared to the time it would take to load each one separately.

When we finished, we separated the loaders and had eight each. That gave us forty-five rounds of buckshot to use on our little friends. Normally, I would use my rifle, but as I thought about the attacks we had seen, and the way the little Z's came at us, precision was a luxury we couldn't afford. Fire a shot at a zombie and it was the only round headed their way. Fine, well and good. If they were slow and you had a chance to aim, you'd likely kill it. With a fast, short zombie, the smarter thing to do was use a gun that threw lots of bullets in the general direction, and you had a good chance of one of them being a killing shot. We didn't have shotguns with us in Iowa, and it may not have made a difference in the long run, but we certainly were going to use them here.

"Coming up to Marsailles," Duncan called out. Charlie and I were just watching the river flow by. We didn't feel the need to talk about anything just yet, and it was nice to just let the river take over our thoughts.

"Keep it going; we need to get to Seneca before we get off," I said. The sun bounced off the water, and created neat light reflections that played along the reeds and trees that lined the banks. I actually found it hard to believe that just this morning, I found my father at my brother's grave. That was only six hours ago, and now we were charging into the woods to take out a threat, but to avenge his death as well.

"Righty ho," Duncan whistled slightly as he drove the boat, giving this whole experience a rather surreal feel to it.

A second thought occurred to me, and I was curious enough finally to ask it out loud.

"Hey, Duncan."

"Yo."

"How do you feel about leaving Janna and your child behind to go fight zombies?"

Duncan turned around slightly to give me a look before continuing his piloting of the boat.

He didn't answer right away, and I worried I may have offended him, but when I thought about that, I realized I couldn't possibly offend him by asking him something that I seemed to do on a regular basis, sadly.

"It sucks, John. It really does. But I know why I do it, and I accept that it's part of what we do. I don't have to, but I do it anyway," Duncan said.

"Okay, I get that, but why do you go?" I was really curious, and maybe I was looking for answers as to why I constantly left, instead of sending others away.

"Simple answer is you, Charlie, and Tommy. You're closer to me than brothers, and I don't think I could stay while you went into danger. If something happened, the question that would always haunt me is whether or not my being there might have made a difference," Duncan said.

I thought about it and it made more sense than anything I could have come up with. I couldn't describe my relationship with my friends. It was more than friendship, more than brotherhood. It was a special kind of bond, and impossible to describe to anyone who had never felt such a thing before.

Whatever thoughts I had about that were interrupted by Duncan announcing we were coming up on Seneca. Charlie and I loaded up our vests with the speed loaders, and filled another for Duncan. I spread out two more boxes of shells in my vest's pockets, and Charlie did the same. Duncan told us he would take care of that himself once we landed. No offense intended, he just didn't trust Charlie's hands in his pockets.

Charlie didn't say anything, but when he stood up, he casually took a swipe at Duncan's head with his hand. Duncan easily ducked it, anticipating Charlie's response. I just shook my head and waited to land the boat.

CHAPTER 34

When we pulled up to the dock, several things were wrong all at the same time. Apparently, the last flood we had did some serious damage to this part of the river, and the dock was one of the casualties. The posts were knocked almost over, and the end of the pier was dipping into the water. Several planks were missing, and there was no way we could use this thing.

"Any ideas?" I said, looking over the damage. Duncan slowed the engine to an idle that kept us in place as the river tried to push us onward.

Charlie nodded. "Duncan, find a spot on the riverbank that you could ground us on." Charlie went back to the bench seats and pulled a length of rope out of the storage unit under the cushions.

"Okay, hang on." Duncan revved the engine and headed upriver, scanning the riverbanks for someplace suitable. What we were doing was difficult, since there was a lot of debris and submerged obstacles that could damage our boat. But after a minute, Duncan found what he was looking for and suddenly angled the boat to the right. Shoving the throttle forward, we lurched towards the side of the river, heading towards a small, rocky beach.

I winced as the metal pontoons screeched up the gravel, halting us abruptly. One of the bikes nearly fell over, which would have been a disaster, since it was the end one and it would have fallen into the water.

Duncan cut the engine and Charlie quickly jumped off the boat and tied the end of the rope he was carrying to a nearby tree. The other end was secured to the back of the pontoon, keeping the vessel steady while we got the bikes off. The front of the boat was going nowhere, and I was slightly worried that it might be permanent, but I couldn't concern myself with that now.

Charlie worked the bikes around on the boat while I went ashore and got my bearings. We were a little bit further east than we needed to be, but were still in good shape. I could see DuPont road from the river, and that's where we needed to get to get to the Marsailles Fish and Wildlife Area. If all went well, we would get there just before the kids and take them out, before they had a chance to scatter.

Just as I was headed back to the boat, I could hear Charlie start up one of the bikes. From the sound of things, it was the CBR, and I was very curious as to his plan of unloading.

There was a loud noise as Charlie revved the engine, then a high-pitched whine, and then a crunch as tires hit the gravel. A second later, Charlie was hurtling past me, bumping over the grass and weeds. Charlie stopped and turned the bike off, grinning like a kid.

"You gotta try that, it's awesome!" he said.

I laughed. "Looks like I should." A second engine started up, and although it wasn't as loud, it definitely had authority. The same progression of events occurred, but this time I ran closer to see, and managed to catch Duncan in mid-flight, as he used the pontoon boat as a ramp and jumped off of the boat, landing on the gravel and speeding up the riverbank. He was faster than Charlie was, and nearly got air a second time as he topped the bank.

Duncan and Charlie grinned like idiots at each other, and then Duncan pointed at the boat. "Your chariot awaits, sirrah."

Shaking my head at the two kinds of fools I chose to work with, I hurried down the bank and into the boat. I straddled the BMW and walked it back into place between the pilot and copilot's seats on the boat. Getting the engine started, I revved it as well, keeping the rear brake locked as I gave it some gas. When I was ready, I released the brake, shooting forward and off the end of the boat. I nearly lost my balance as I landed, and managed to wobble my way over the edge of the riverbank.

I joined Charlie and Duncan, and together we made our way to the river road, carefully dodging debris. When the river flooded, this part always caught some of it, and without crews to clear the way, there was a lot of dead wood and dried out seaweed. There was other debris here as well, and if you looked hard enough, you'd find quite a few remains of people whose last refuge from the dead became their grave.

To the south of us, the forest was huge. It was an area bigger than our own forest, and to the south of that, was the nuclear power plant and cooling lake. The plant still supplied a lot of power to several towns, and we were lucky to have found a person who survived the Upheaval to have worked there. They stayed nearby and kept the plant running, although at limited capacity.

We rode as quickly as we could to the forest, and once there, we stopped at a small information center. The place was long abandoned, but looked to be in decent shape. English ivy was growing over a good portion of it, covering about a third from one end to the other.

We shut the bikes off and I walked over to the center. From my vantage point, I could see into the visitor area, and realized there was nothing of use in there. I was looking for a map, and said so out loud to my companions.

"What about that?" Duncan asked, pointing to a sign about a hundred feet away. It was located slightly out of the way, but I realized that it was on a trail, just an overgrown one.

"Perfect." I went over quickly and after a cursory glance, found that the park was laid out just as I had hoped. There were several trails, but they all interconnected and they were all loops. They all connected to a center trail. It was like a cargo net of trails and would serve nicely. I looked down the first trail, and was relieved to see it was still there. It was smaller than when it first began, and eventually would fade away altogether, but for now, it was enough.

I looked at Charlie and Duncan. "This one's going to be tough. We are going to need to be sharp to make this work. Stay on your bikes, and keep moving. If you go down, get to a tree and get climbing. We'll save you later. Mike made a sizable dent in these bastards, and I want to finish the job. Any questions?"

"Why didn't we just take the truck over here?" Duncan wanted to know.

Before I answered, Charlie snapped his fingers. "The trails. Nice thinking."

Duncan looked confused. "I'm still lost."

"Never mind," I said, laughing. "Let's get this moving. I'll take the southern end of the forest, Charlie, you're in the middle, and Duncan, you're north. Let's keep a sharp eye and stay in contact. First one who sees movement lets the others know before engaging. Let's move."

CHAPTER 35

We rode carefully through the forest, keeping a sharp eye on the trails. The paths were covered with leaves in spots, and it didn't take too many leaves to cause a bike to slip. Here and there, animals scurried out of our way, and more than one family of ground squirrels bolted for cover at the sight of the metal monsters invading their domain.

Duncan broke off and stopped, and in my rear view mirror I could see him setting up the bike, scouting for a good position, and he would be checking his ammo and shotgun in due order. Goofy as he could be, Duncan was a fighter.

About halfway in, Charlie slowed and stopped, and I gave a wave as I left him behind. I worried and didn't worry about Charlie, if that made any sense. He could die, just as I could, but it would take some serious killing to get it done.

About five minutes later, I reached the southernmost loop of the trail and found a place for the bike. I was going to leave it on idle, since I didn't want to have to start it up, but I decided to leave it off just for noise. I figured I would start it when I saw the zombies, since they'd be seeing me as well.

I called on the radio to Charlie and Duncan, and got 'All clear' from them both. The hardest part about this game was the waiting. It gave me too much time to think about things, and inevitably, my thoughts drifted back to my brother. The unfairness of it all was galling, and I felt extremely guilty for not being there when he died. I felt guilty for waiting so long to rejoin the fight, but I was tired of fighting.

The forest settled down after I turned off the BMW. I pulled the shotgun around and put the sling over my shoulder and neck. I wanted it in front of me at all times for the next few hours. My backpack was in place, and my other weapons were easily at hand. The only thing I didn't have was my rifle, but Tommy was carrying that to Leport.

The sun was a little past its high point, so the trees let in a decent amount of light. The underbrush was thick, but not impassable. I was hoping the zombies would come straight

LAST STAND OF THE DEAD

through, but we'd see them from our positions if they opted to go around. All around me, I could hear rustlings as the animals got used to my presence and treated me as part of the forest. The leaves were turning, getting ready to carpet the forest floor once again in preparation for the winter months. The only thing that kept the trails somewhat clear was the fact that the winds off the river could be strong, and they blew through these trails with enough regularity to keep them pretty clear. We had the same thing happen at Starved Rock. The trails stayed clear most times, and only needed maintenance on a semi-regular basis.

I kept my eyes on the tall grass in the distance, figuring the zombies would be coming from that direction. I also kept a watch on what the animals were doing. If they ran for cover or ran in my direction, I knew the zombies were coming.

"Anything out of sorts on anyone else's end?" I asked quietly on the radio.

Charlie answered first. "All quiet. Couple of rabbits are at the edge of a small clearing in from of me. If they bolt, I'll know something else."

"All clear up here," Duncan said. "Thought I heard a truck on the road, but couldn't see anything."

"It's possible. First one to see anything, calls out, and then keeps it quiet." I said.

"Well, duh," Charlie replied.

I laughed. "Got me on that one. Talon out."

The minutes stretched into an hour, and I was beginning to wonder if we were too late. But just as I was trying to figure out our next move, Charlie's voice came over the radio, quiet as a whisper.

"They're here."

I started the cycle, grateful I had the BMW, which was a quiet running bike to begin with. The idle was quiet as well, but the forest went quiet around me at the metallic sounds.

The wind rustled the leaves, masking the sound of the bike, and I eased the bike into first gear, wincing at the small click that motion caused. I kept one hand on the clutch as I positioned the shotgun, figuring to run and gun. I pointed the bike north and eased up on the clutch, slowly moving forward.

121

Suddenly my radio came alive with the sound of Duncan's voice.

"Are you sure? We're clear up here."

Oh, shit. The last thing I heard on the radio was Charlie cursing at Duncan.

"You idiot."

The next sound I heard as I pulled on the throttle was gunshots.

CHAPTER 36

I didn't stick around to hear Duncan's response. I raced north, hoping I would not be too late. As I got within fifty yards of where I thought Charlie was, I saw a huge group of zombie kids racing around a large tree. Smoke blasted down from the center of the leaves, flattening several zombie kids. I pulled the clutch again, and this time grabbed the shotgun with my right hand. Aiming about where I could find little heads, I launched several rounds towards the horde, being rewarded with at least three knockdowns. Fifty yards was about the range of effectiveness I could expect from a shotgun and buckshot.

Of course, this turned all of their attention to me, even though Charlie used the respite to reload and launch another broadside from the foliage. I reloaded and pulled away as the front line charged me, easing up on the clutch and heading away to a deeper part of the forest. I wanted them to chase me, to draw them away from Charlie.

As I moved, I heard three more shots, then the sound of a CBR firing up. I knew then Charlie was safe, and I had the majority after me. I rode slowly enough to keep the zombies running, but I couldn't turn around, shoot, and take a few out. I crossed a side path and nearly turned north, but in the next couple of seconds, I was glad I didn't.

From the left came Duncan and he was blazing like a bat out of hell. He must have been going thirty miles an hour, a risky proposition in the forest of leaves and branches. His left hand held the shotgun, with the barrel riding alongside the windshield. Duncan fired as he came within range, splitting the horde in half. He kept moving, and slammed into a small boy who flew through the air, bouncing off a tree, and lying still at the base. Duncan corrected the slide that was caused and stopped about forty yards away to reload. One push and he was ready to go again, but he chose to ride away to the south, much to my chagrin.

I stopped my bike, and spun around, punching a large hole through the head of the little demon who was about to launch himself at me. He was the closest, and I shot the next two that were edging up on me. Two more shots in the general direction of the horde and then I reloaded and was gone.

The zombies kept coming, having only me to chase, when Charlie showed up from the south. He came out of the woods like a vengeful god, firing as he went, and when he reached the main horde, he used his shotgun as a club and knocked one down as he passed. That little girl hissed loudly as she regained her feet, only to lose her footing as Duncan returned and shot her in the head. Four more shots and he was gone again, disappearing to the north. Several zombies broke off and followed him, which wasn't a good thing, but there wasn't anything I could do about it now. I just kept heading east, drawing the main horde with me, hoping to see Charlie again.

Just then, Charlie reappeared. He followed the same pattern, firing into the crowd, and running into another kid that got in his way. It would have worked, too, except the kid was kind of large and got caught up in the area between the engine and the front forks. Charlie couldn't dislodge him, and ended up putting the bike on its side, jumping clear as the bike spun off the road and into a tree.

"Charlie! Run for it!" I yelled, firing at the horde again. I thought we'd be able to handle this, when suddenly the zombies disappeared.

I was speechless for a second, not understanding what was happening, when Charlie called out.

"They're stalking! They just ducked down. Meet me over on the trail!" Charlie bolted, running like he was late for dinner.

As I swung the bike around, I could hear the clicking of teeth that always accompanied an attack. I wondered if it was just a herd thing or something worse. The tall grass concealed the zombies pretty well, but if you looked, you could see the tall weeds and grasses parting as the deadly little hunters made their way forward. I resisted the temptation to fire, since it would just be a waste of ammo.

Charlie reached the trail ahead of me, and was waiting with his gun up, ready to kill anything that showed its ugly face. I raced over, and covered the ground as he situated himself on the back of the bike. He faced backwards, and used the slings from the shotguns to rig a makeshift harness for himself. This took longer than I was hoping for and the Z's attacked again as we were sitting there.

Charlie fired five times, and then I fired while he reloaded. I reloaded while he fired, then I fired again. We were making some good progress knocking this horde down to size when they suddenly shifted and ran to the north.

"Dammit! How do they know when to cut and run?" Charlie complained as he reloaded again.

"I think these little suckers run on pure instinct, and when they feel they can't fight, they take flight," I said, reloading again. I had four speed loaders left, and I took a second to fill two empty ones.

Charlie didn't say anything for a minute, taking a second to reload a couple of his speed loaders as well. When he did speak, I was surprised.

"That's probably the most accurate thing about these little bastards I've heard so far," He said, complimenting me. "Let's find Duncan."

Gunshots to the south told us the direction to travel, so I kicked the bike into gear and headed that way. It took me a minute to get used to the extra weight on the bike, and to be perfectly honest, Charlie was a tough passenger to have. He was built like me, with most of his weight on his chest and shoulders, which put the point of balance on the BMW very high. On a hard turn, we'd go down in a heartbeat. Add leaves to the equation and I'd be surprised if we weren't walking in ten minutes.

We moved slowly through the trees, hoping to catch sight of our little friends. I would be happy to catch sight of our larger friend Duncan, but since I still heard the occasional shot, I knew he was still in the fight.

CHAPTER 37

Charlie tapped me on the shoulder and pointed to the trail ahead. I stopped the bike and we both got off. I moved forward and slipped into the lighter brush by the trail. Charlie was on the other side of the trail, and moved as quietly as I did. Ahead of us, a small group of ten zombies was moving slowly our way. Had we kept riding, we would have plowed right into them.

I looked over at Charlie, and signaled for him to get higher. I scrambled up a nearby tree that had a branch about eight feet off the ground. It stretched out over the trail, but I was content to lean against the tree and straddle the branch. Charlie found a spot directly across from me, but a little lower to the ground. Since we were across from each other, we had to get higher. This way, we could shoot in the other's direction and not worry about hitting each other.

The zombies advanced, moving slowly, looking in all directions. They seemed unconcerned with the shotgun blasts that were coming out of the woods around them, focusing only on the motorcycle sitting in the middle of the path. There were eight of them, in various states of decay and raggedness. Two of them didn't have shirts, but they didn't have ears either, the cause which I didn't want to think about.

Charlie looked over at me and I signaled him by sticking out four fingers and moving my hand across my chest to the left. Charlie nodded. I was telling him I was going to take the four to the left when they came into view, and he was going to take the four to the right.

I waited until the small band passed us, and when the middle kid was directly below, I cut loose on the four leaders to my left. On my signal, Charlie blasted away on his side.

My first two shots cut down the zombies without warning, and the rest of the gang looked around for a second before trying to move. That second was fatal, as it allowed me to shift my aim and fire three more times. I dropped the last of my side a second before

Charlie dropped his. One of his managed to turn and start a run for the brush, but the buckshot ended those intentions.

I reloaded and clambered down the tree, trying not to hurt myself in the process, and looked over our prey. Three of them were still moving, two of mine and one of Charlie's. Their heads were shifting, but the rest of them was quiet, telling me that they had large lead balls lodged in their spines. I took out my pick and finished them off, pulling out a lighter to burn off the virus. Charlie smacked the life out of his, and then burned his hawk as well.

We stood for a minute, listening carefully to the woods. We didn't hear any movement, or any teeth for that matter, and I actually took this as a good sign. We didn't have an accurate count as to how many of them there were, so we had no way of knowing if we'd killed them all. All I could hope for was the chance that some of my brother's killers were dead at my feet.

"Come on, let's go find Duncan," I said, heading back to the motorcycle. The BMW had just sat through the whole thing, purring contentedly while it waited for us to return. We mounted up and moved again towards the sounds of conflict.

Three minutes later and we were off the bike again, moving quietly through the brush. From where we were, we could see Duncan sitting in a tree, contentedly killing the occasional zombie when they tried to move around him. He saw us coming through the grass and started to make some more noise, keeping our arrival quiet from the zombies in the tall grass. I didn't think he could carry a tune, and Charlie's face reflected the same thought when Duncan started up a rousing rendition of "Crazy Train."

The kids thought it was awesome, with several of them running up to the tree and raised their arms in adoration. I'm sure he would be very well received if he tried body-surfing across that little sea of terror.

Charlie and I used the distraction to spread apart, approaching the tree through the brush. I stepped over several bodies, and hoped the group we had here was the last.

I waved at Charlie, and then got my reloads ready. I was going to use everything I had, and figured Charlie would, too.

Charlie and I opened fire at the same time. The kids were confused, not understanding where the firing was coming from. I cut down several children, aiming at their necks and heads, shoving five more rounds in my gun after the mag went dry. Charlie spaced his shots a little wider, and we managed to keep the noise up pretty well. Duncan just took cover in the crotch of the tree, and waited for the firing to die down.

After two minutes of killing, we stopped to assess the damage. The Z's didn't have a single point to focus on, so they just milled for minute, giving us the opportunity to cut them down.

"How's it look, Duncan?" Charlie called.

"Looks like nap time at a day care," Duncan said.

"You're sick."

"Probably. But you know...oh shit. Get down!" Duncan yelled, pulling up his gun.

Charlie and I hit the deck, learning a long time ago to trust every member of our crew implicitly. If anyone ever said 'Duck', or 'Jump,' you did so without hesitation. I dropped to a knee in the tall grass and hunched low, effectively hiding from anything not three feet away from me. I quietly checked my pockets for shotgun shells, and was relieved to find ten left. I reloaded my Benelli and one speed loader, and waited for Duncan to fill me in.

Duncan didn't disappoint. "There's sixteen more, coming through the trees to the north," he said quietly. There was enough of a breeze and enough leaves rustling around that his words didn't carry much further than us. "They're spreading out, moving slowly."

"John, slide to the west. Keep going. Keep going. Right there."

Duncan waited, watching the zombie kids moving slowly towards us. I was sweating. If they came across me, I'd have no time to get into action before they overwhelmed me.

"Charlie, head south. Other way, dipshit," Duncan chided.

I couldn't be sure, but I thought I heard a whispered "Fucker!" from Charlie's end of the woods.

"Here they come. I'll try and get their...*shit*!" Duncan yelled, and there was a crashing sound and a heavy expelling of air.

This time I know I heard the word "Idiot!" because I was the one that said it. There was no other explanation for what had happened. Duncan had fallen out of the damn tree.

CHAPTER 38

The noise caused the zombies to go into attack mode, and we could hear the clicking of their teeth as they advanced. I slowly raised my head and was level with the top of the grass. To the north, there was a lot of grass swaying in the wind, and not all of the movement was caused by air.

I caught a bit of movement to the south and Charlie's head peeked above the grass. He gave me a small wave, and then ducked back down. At least I knew where he was. Duncan stood up behind the tree, using it as cover as he stood and stretched his back. He exhaled slowly to the sky, and then inhaled slowly, a sure sign the wind had been knocked out of him. That probably saved his life, since it shut him up. Had he called out, the zombies would have been all over him like ants on a cough drop.

Duncan saw me looking, nodded, pulled out his sword, crouched down, and I could see him heading towards the zombies.

I gave it a second thought, and then figured it would be the best plan. Instead of waiting for them to come to us, and possibly getting surrounded, we were going to go to them. I liked this much better. I wanted to close in to my brother's killers and cut them down face to face. The more I thought about Mike, the more I started to get angry, and the cold fires started again.

I held my knife in my left hand, keeping my 'hawk in my right. I slipped further north, hoping to come around them from the back and take them out as they moved in front of me. The clicking kept up, which actually helped a great deal in determining where the little bastards were.

Tall grass parted in front of me, and I used the long blade of my knife to lead the way. I moved quickly, circling around and coming up from the rear. When I thought I was about in the middle of their formation, I moved south, keeping an ear out for any movement to my left or right. It would be downright embarrassing to stalk these kids so well that I wound up in the middle of them.

I moved forward carefully and heard something directly in front of me. I took a quick peek above the grass and was rewarded with the sight of a small boy turning around to look directly at me. His eyes were bloodshot and rimmed with dark tissue, giving him an obscene look. His nostrils flared and his mouth opened, showing me bits of decaying flesh stuck in his teeth.

He started to turn and my hand shot forward, spearing one of those awful eyes right to the hilt. The curve of my knife swept the blade into the brain, and I gave the knife a reflexive twist. I pulled the boy back towards me and caught the back of his neck, easing him to the ground. I had to be careful when I grabbed him, since I didn't want to stab myself with a knife that was covered in bits of brain.

I slowly eased the knife out, wiping it off on the Z's dirty shirt. I moved forward again, a little more quickly, seeking another target. This time it was a girl about ten years old, and she never saw me coming. I stabbed her in the back of the neck and let her momentum pull her off my blade.

I stepped forward some more, and then suddenly stopped. The clicking had ceased, and I didn't want to be too far forward if they discovered me. I waited in the tall grass, listening intently. I didn't hear anything moving, so I didn't want to be the only one making noise and become a target.

Suddenly the air was split by a huge bellow. "*John!*"

It was Charlie. I stood up and saw Charlie standing in a small cleared area, surrounded by zombies, who were advancing slowly. Charlie couldn't shoot, because Duncan and I would be in the line of fire. I did the only thing I could think of to do.

I hurled my trench hawk, burying the blade in the back of the head of one of the zombies. I sheathed my knife as I ran forward, pulling my .45 from its holster. If I was close enough, I could shoot more at a downward angle, reducing the chance of shooting Charlie or Duncan.

"Here, you bastards!" Duncan suddenly yelled, standing up and brandishing his sword. It was bloodied from mid-blade to tip, and Duncan held it like a baseball bat, practically daring the Z's to attack him.

That distraction turned a few heads, and I took the opportunity to shoot three of them down. The noise spun their heads back to me, and Charlie stepped forward to kill two of them. Duncan rushed the two coming at him, and he cut them down without mercy. One leaped at me, but I dodged to the side, bringing my gun around and firing at its head at point-blank range as it passed by. The extra push threw the small body through the grass like a rag doll. I swung the gun around but by this time, Charlie had his out and was firing as well. He killed three on his right side, and I finished off one that was moving away to the tree line.

Charlie and I waited with our backs towards each other as Duncan scrambled up the tree he had fallen out of. He leaned out over our position and gave us the all clear before losing his grip and falling to the ground again. This time he was ready and only managed to jam the hilt of his sword into his side as he landed.

"That it?" Charlie asked, wiping off his tomahawks and knife.

I nodded. "I think we did it. If there are any more, they've gone."

"How do you think the others are doing?" Duncan asked.

I shook my head. "No way to know. But we'd better get ourselves moving and find a place for the night. We should be well north by noon tomorrow."

"Are we riding or floating?" Charlie asked.

I hadn't thought about it. If we were riding, we'd be able to address any further outbreaks. On the other hand, the boat would get us to Leport that much faster and a much more direct route. Then again, the bikes were a *lot* faster and we'd make it there quicker along an indirect route.

"Let's get the bikes. Charlie, you think the CBR is road-worthy?" I asked, remembering Charlie had put the bike down earlier.

"Only one way to find out," Charlie said. "Duncan, give me a lift, hey?"

"Surely, surely," Duncan said, turning and heading out of the woods. He had left the bike in between a couple of trees, and it only took a second to get fired up. I ran back to the other BMW and we all rode carefully back to where Charlie first put the CBR down. The bike was scraped to hell and back on one side, but the front forks were fine and the tires were still good. The clutch handle was bent a little outwards, but Charlie said he could reach it just fine. The bike was still on, but the battery had enough power to turn over. Charlie got it started on the fourth try, revving the engine and checking the systems for damage.

When he was satisfied, he gave Duncan and me the thumbs up, and we turned our bikes north and then headed east, following the river until it turned further north. We had no option but to cross or head east, and I didn't want to cross just yet. I knew there were a lot of things going on up north, and I didn't want to find myself in the middle of it just yet. The plan was to head to Leport, and that was what we were going to do. Besides, I had another plan to get through, and it was to the east of us.

CHAPTER 39

I opened up the BMW and raced along the farm road, going as quickly as I could. Strangely enough, farm roads survived the seasons better than the 'well-travelled' roads. It made sense, since farm roads weren't maintained as often, nor travelled as often. I followed a zigzag pattern through the underbelly of the Illinois River, passing signs for Morris and Heidecke Lake. I cruised along Pine Bluff Road, coming to a stop outside the entrance to Goose Lake Prairie State Park. A truck was parked by the entrance, and two men were sitting on the tailgate arguing over a map.

I pulled up about twenty feet from the truck, nodding at Charlie and Duncan. Those two got off their bikes and stood apart from me, about where I needed them in case of an ambush. Charlie kept his right thumb hooked in his belt about an inch from his gun, and Duncan stood with his hands inside the armholes of his vest. If you didn't know better, Duncan looked like he was just relaxing without a care in the world. In fact, he actually had his hands on two small pistols which were resting in holsters sewn into the inside of his vest. In the blink of an eye, Duncan could have two guns out and firing before you even knew he was armed.

I walked apart from my cycle, circling wide to keep it out of the line of fire. The men on the truck continued to argue about the map, and I just laughed out loud.

"Has it been that long, Andre?" I called over.

The dark haired man on the right broke into a huge grin. "That it has, John, that it has." He let go of his side of the map, showing me the gun he was holding in his other hand. He hopped off the bed of the truck and limped over to me, where he wrapped his big arms around me in a fierce hug.

The man on the left jumped off and scampered over to Charlie and Duncan, giving hugs to both. "Good to see you, boys! Good to see you!"

Charlie and Duncan returned the favor, with Duncan asking questions.

"Where you living now? What's happening in the south? Any outbreaks?" He said.

Kyle, the dark haired man, answered in his broken way. "We're south of here, 'bout 40 mile. No breaks, just farm. That's all. Just farm." Kyle was a man of few words, but he was a deadly fighter. He was part of the group of veterans that had fought with me all the way to Colorado. He was an engineer who helped close the gaps in the mountains, sealing off the West Coast forever. His speech was a result of a car accident many years ago.

I returned the hug to Andre before asking some questions of my own. "How's things? You okay?"

Andre looked down. "Beth died last winter. Pneumonia. Hard to believe after all we went through."

I put a hand on his shoulder. "I'm sorry, man. She was a good woman. How are the kids? They okay?"

Andre smiled a bit. "They're better. We're busy with the farm and the forge, so that helps." Andre was an amateur blacksmith who happened to have a talent with metal. His knives and weapons were sought after, and he did well in his trade. Charlie's tomahawks were made by Andre last year, replacing the ones that had been with him for so long. Andre's were better balanced, flew farther, and kept their edges longer. Couldn't ask for more, as Charlie said...

Andre looked at me. "What are we facing, John Talon?"

I got down to business. "We're heading north to the capital, trying to hook up with as many veterans as would answer the call. The zombies we're facing are not like anything you've seen before."

Andre held up a hand. "Hold on, we all need to hear this." He put his hand to his mouth and blew out a strong whistle. Fifteen men and nine women emerged from the trees, all well-armed and well-equipped.

I smiled in spite of myself, and was rewarded with big grins and smiles in return. I knew all of these men and women, and felt almost relief in having them with me. If this group had accompanied us to Iowa, the threat would have died there, no question about it.

I spent several minutes shaking hands and giving hugs, and one woman threw her arms around me and gave me a huge kiss.

"That's better!" said the buxom blonde attached to me. "How you been, John? You still married or have I finally gotten lucky?" she asked saucily.

I put the woman down gently. "Sarah's fine, Donna. She misses you, too."

"Arrgh, why did she see you first?" Donna growled. She was a tall woman, with generous curves, and a beautiful, care-lined face. In her day, she was probably stunning, but time and worry had taken a small toll in wrinkles and creases. She ran a farm down south, and when the Upheaval had hit, she took it upon herself to take in every orphan she could find or fight for, whose parents had succumbed to the disease or zombies. When I met her, she had forty-seven kids on her fifty-acre farm, and was managing to care for all of them. She joined our effort across the country, for no other reason than to take care of the children we found. There wasn't a man alive who wouldn't defend Donna to the death for what she had done.

I gave Donna an extra hug, with a butt squeeze thrown in to make her squeak. She swatted my hand, but didn't knife me, for which I was grateful.

When the catching up was quickly finished, I took the map and outlined what we had been doing and where we had been. I described everything to the veterans, right down to the death of my brother. Several heads went down at that news, as Mike was a well-liked man. They were especially quiet when I described the zombies, shaking their heads at what the Z's could do and how they were doing it. I finished quickly, and we mapped out a route to the capital.

"I think we killed off the horde that was south of the river, but I don't have a way of being sure," I said honestly. "I don't know how many attacked the lodge or how many might have splintered off. If there are any more, then they went further south. I don't have the time to look for them."

Donna raised a hand. "I don't think I could kill them, John. I just don't know."

Andre patted her arm. "They stopped being kids when they became zombies, you know that."

Donna nodded and let it go. I continued.

"Right now we need to get to 53 and head north. I figure we can pass by Joslin without any trouble, and head up through Freeport, reaching Leport from the south end. Tommy, Sarah, and Rebecca are meeting up with veterans on the north side of the river, hoping to engage and guide the zombies towards the 355 bridge. If we're lucky, they'll take the bait and try and engage us on the bridge." I looked at the map. "Bad luck would have us making preparations for one bridge and they end up on another."

I rolled up the map. "Any questions?"

One hand rose above the rest. I looked for a second, and then suppressed a laugh.

"Yes, Duncan?" I asked patiently.

"Can I go to the bathroom?"

"No. Anyone else?" I asked the group of chuckling men and women. "All right, let's get this done. And everyone?" I said, turning people's heads my way. "I sure am glad to see each and every one of you."

Charlie, Duncan and I went back to our motorcycles and fired them up. Charlie popped me on the arm.

"Think we got 'em?" he asked, readying himself for a ride.

"Hope so, old friend. Hope so." I tried to sound convincing, but deep inside, the fear of getting others killed was starting to grow and chew into my gut with tiny icicles for teeth.

CHAPTER 40

We moved north as quickly as we could, three motorcycles moving a convoy of cars, trucks, and trailers. I would have liked to be able to reach Leport before nightfall, but I knew it was impossible. We were too far south and too deep in the sticks to find roads that would take us north fast enough.

As it was, we were able to secure some night lodging in a casino just south of Joslin. Charlie and three of the other men checked the place out, and declared it safe. The rest of us went inside, and I was stunned at how pristine the place was. It looked like it was ready to open the very next day. The place was dusty, but not bad, and the tables and slots were all covered in plastic. Tommy pulled the cover off of one slot machine and it gleamed in the thin light of the flashlights.

"What's your game, John?" Duncan asked, walking around a dormant roulette table.

I shook my head. "Craps was my game. My brother and I would celebrate each other's birthdays by going out to dinner and hitting a casino afterwards." I ran my hand over the side of a craps table. "It was a good little tradition." I said softly.

"Well, times change." Donna said, pulling the cover off of another craps table. "Right now, these tables are a good place to sleep, dust-free."

I couldn't argue with that, and soon enough, all of the craps tables and roulette tables were occupied with men and women spreading out their blankets and bags. Andre pushed two blackjack tables together, and Duncan made a bed out of bar chairs. I had a craps table myself, and I lay my head down among the high dollar chips I always chased, but never seemed to catch.

The night crept up on us, and I was surprised at how tired I suddenly was. I lay quietly among the lines of the craps table, and I was humorously struck with how ironic it was that I was in a place that required luck, and here I was, someone who at times had denied its existence.

Suddenly, Donna's head popped up over the edge of the table.

"Hey, Handsome! You want to try your luck?" Donna said with a wicked leer.

I chuckled. "Oh, Lordy. No, I think I'll keep my life, thanks."

"Just a figure of speech, just a figure a speech. Seriously, though, you got room in there?" Without waiting for a reply, Donna slipped over the side of the table and lay down next to me. I shifted to my side to make room for her, and she lay on her side facing me.

"Truth talk, John," Donna whispered.

"As you wish," I whispered back.

"What are we really facing here?"

I considered the question and who was asking it. "It's probably your worst nightmare, Donna. These are just little kids, from about twelve years old to around four or five. But they stalk you, they ambush you, and they wait for you to make a mistake. They can communicate on a basic level, and they have a kind of instinctual fight or flight mechanism. If they can't win, or face overwhelming odds, they flee. Simple as that."

Donna mulled it over for a while. "I don't know, John. I don't know if I can kill them. I might hesitate long enough to let one of them get to me, and then where would my kids be?"

I thought of a different tack. "You are actually fighting for your kids. This group we're chasing isn't the original. They've recruited all along their path to here."

"What do you mean, 'recruited'?"

"Every town they've attacked, they either bite the kids or carry them off to bite them later. If they win, and then head south, all of your kids could be in danger."

Donna shuddered. "Oh, Jesus, John. Now what do I do? If I go, then you're short handed. If I stay, then my kids are defenseless."

I didn't envy her choice, so I tried to make it easier. "Where would you have a better chance of survival? Here among all of us, the best the Upheaval could produce. Or down home, where you'd be by yourself? How long could you hold out against a smart, determined, fast, dead enemy?"

Donna thought for a second. "Well, when you put it that way..." She turned away and scooted towards me, reaching behind her for my arm which she promptly wrapped around her healthy chest. "Night, John."

I lay my head down my other arm, content to breathe onto the back of Donna's neck until I fell asleep.

I woke up in the middle of night, still wrapped up with Donna. I don't know what caused me to wake, but I listened very carefully to the small sounds all around me. I could make out Duncan's high-pitched snoring, and on the other end of the spectrum, I could hear Charlie's deep, bellows-like breathing. Donna seemed not to be breathing at all, but I could feel her chest rise and fall against my forearm. Not hearing anything I couldn't place, I went back to sleep.

CHAPTER 41

In the morning, I woke to the sound of movement all around me. Men and women were gathering up their things, and Donna was off getting herself ready for the day. I took a drink of water from my bottle and used a little to wash the sleep out of my eyes. A quick bathroom break and we were assembling in the foyer that led to the outside parking lot.

The sun was just coming up over the horizon, casting the clouds in brilliant shades of red and orange. The river behind us added a low mist to the picture, blotting out the parking lot in a gray, swirling vapor. Behind the parking lot was a huge forest, and it was clear the forest had its eyes on taking over the asphalt, since roots and tendrils reached out all along the border of the lot.

I started to say something when Charlie held up a hand. He had been staring out at the mist for a while, so he must have seen something out of the ordinary. Everyone moved back into the shadows, with weapons coming up and safeties being switched off. Three of the group slipped over to the right side of the door while three more moved to the left. The rest took up positions in the rear, overlapping their fields of fire in case of a break in. God, it was nice to work with professionals again.

"Talk to me," I said, not moving a muscle.

"Four of them, far end of the lot, two males and two females."

"You loaded?" I asked, referring to his shotgun.

"All ready."

I looked back for a second. "There's four of them out there. Charlie and I will go and get them. Cover us from the rear; we'll try to draw them closer."

I didn't wait for a reply because I wasn't going to get one. We knew what to do and how to do it. I reminded myself once again that this was a good crew to work with. Then again, the crew I worked with before got killed by these monsters as well.

That comforting thought accompanied me out to the parking lot as I held my shotgun out in front of me. We all could die, if we didn't get this under control.

Out in the parking area, things were amazingly quiet. I could hear the river behind us, as I could hear the sounds of the forest next to us. Across the way, I could see the zombies moving at an easy walk. I doubted they even knew where they were going, and left to themselves, they'd probably walk until their feet fell off, or they hit water, and moved along the bank until they came to a bridge. They were smarter than the average zombie was, but they weren't that smart.

I crouched and moved to the left, trying to stay out of sight for a few seconds. The mist was about waist high, and thick. I could see through it to about fifteen feet in front of me, but after that, it obscured my vision effectively. Once in place, I sent a hand signal to Charlie, who had moved off to the right. He was crouched as well. Out of the corner of my eye, I could see the rest of the men and women watching from the doorway. I only hoped I didn't trip or my fly wasn't open before we opened up the dance.

Charlie raised a hand, and at the signal, I stood up and called out.

"Hey, over here!"

The change was nearly instantaneous. The four of them turned their heads, then ducked low, coming right for me. They weren't much taller than the mist, so when they crouched down, their heads were just under the surface. The swirling vapor parted as they rushed through it, swiftly hurrying in my direction. The effect from where I was standing was like watching some large fish moving towards you in water. For a second, I felt like a cow that had fallen in the Amazon River.

When the zombies were halfway to me, Charlie called out on his side.

"How about over here?"

The zombies stopped suddenly, and two heads popped up from the fog. They oriented on Charlie, and I thought they were going to head his way, when they ducked back down and all four kept heading right towards me.

Really? I thought as I brought up my shotgun. Thank God, I wasn't going to try and do this with a rifle. I waited until the swirling mist was about twenty feet away before I opened fire.

Shogun blasts crashed through the air as I opened up on the Z's. I aimed where I thought their heads might be, and fired all of my rounds as quickly as possible. I grabbed a reloader and shoved the rounds in, losing precious seconds as the mist swirled closer and closer.

Charlie came to the rescue, blasting the area with his shotgun. The buckshot whipping through the fog caused swirls, which created openings to see through. I could see one down, and another crawling. A third was coming closer, and I let him have it in the face with a blast. That finished him. The fourth was nowhere to be seen, and Charlie shot down the second one on the ground.

I waved Charlie back, not wanting to take the risk of getting bit while this fog was around us. We moved slowly, easing our way to the entrance doors. Charlie and I both scanned the fog, but we couldn't see anything out of the ordinary. I knew the little shit was in there somewhere, but I had no way of flushing him out.

I decided on another tactic, one that Sarah would kill me for if she ever found out. I motioned Charlie to go inside, and he raised a curious eyebrow at me. Waving him in, I knelt down and started to whistle. Not being the creative kind like Duncan, I just carried an impromptu tune across the drifting mist.

In a minute, I heard it. The telltale clicking of a zombie, hunting its prey. I couldn't explain it to anyone why they did it, any more than I could explain why they were the way they were. It just happened, and we dealt with it.

There was an odd echo off of the parking garage to the east, but I didn't pay it any mind as I watched the mists swirl in front of me. I held the shotgun; very much aware I only had a few shots left. We had depleted our supplies pretty well, but I knew our rifles and more ammo was waiting for us in Leport, so I didn't worry about it too much.

The clicking stopped, and I knew the little shit was close. I wished the sun would come out suddenly and fry off the mist, but even if it did, it would still not be enough to see by. I let out a long breath, not whistling this time. I was sweating in my clothes. There was ten feet of visible space between the fog and myself, and that wasn't a lot of time to get things done.

The mist swirled suddenly in front of me causing me to swing the muzzle and fire into the fog. The blast parted the vapor for a moment, revealing absolutely naught. I shook my head at myself because I was shooting at shadows.

I fretted for a minute, and then decided against moving. I figured they would come to me soon enough. I waited, and watched. The rising sun turned the grey mist white, and I could see a small shape standing next to one of the massive yellow pillars holding up the giant awning which stretched out into the parking area. I lined up the ghost ring sight, waiting for the opportunity to fire. For all I knew at this point, I was aiming at a plant.

The form shifted, and I thought it was nothing, when it suddenly ducked low and raced at me. I shifted my aim slightly and pulled the trigger, the recoil of the shotgun shoving my shoulder back. The little zombie's head snapped back, catching at least three or four of the buckshot. The momentum of its legs swung the lower half of its body upward, and the back-flung head carried the rest into a backwards somersault. I didn't often impress myself with my shooting, but that one was pretty cool.

The shotgun's slide locked back, and I quickly felt my pockets for more ammo. Not finding any, I placed the shotgun on the ground and started pulling the reloading tubes out of my pockets. I had all of them out and on the ground when they attacked.

Three little zombies flew out of the fog at full speed, their little mouths open and hissing, while their black eyes glared hatred and hunger at me. Their hands were stretched out in front, and their legs burned up the distance between us.

I whipped out my pick with my left hand, using the momentum of drawing it to slam it into the head of the nearest and center zombie. I let the handle go as I drew my trench hawk with my right hand, swinging the spike end up into the temple of the small boy attacking on the right. My left hand wasn't idle while I was killing this zombie, since the one on the left was nearly on top of me. I drew my knife in an awkward cross-body draw, just managing to get the blade reversed and into the head of the third one. Its momentum brought it into me, and as it died, it looked up into my eyes. For the briefest of seconds, I looked into what made these kids monsters, and it was a very frightening thing.

I pulled my weapons from the heads of these three as the doors behind me opened up. Men and women stepped around me and looked down at the bodies. The way they looked now, you would have thought they were just sleeping.

"Jesus, John." Andre spoke first.

"What?" I didn't think I had done anything wrong.

"I think you've actually gotten better," Donna said, standing next to me, looking down at the bodies. Her eyes were misty, and I knew she was thinking about the kids back at her house.

There was assenting murmuring going on around me, which always had always made me uncomfortable. I never sought the limelight, never looked for accolades. I just survived.

"Good work. Next time, keep the help," Charlie admonished as he complimented me. It was a weird combination.

"Well, it's done, and you guys saw how fast they are and how they can ambush. If anyone wants to head home, now's the time." I said, gathering up my stuff. I took out a lighter and burned my weapons. No one paid any attention to the red flames. We'd seen it so often it wasn't even interesting anymore.

Donna spoke, still not taking her eyes off the kids. "I don't think I can do it, John. I don't think I can kill them. I've always had a problem with the kids, and this just makes it worse. I can't be where I might hesitate and get someone else killed. I need to be at home to protect my own in case you guys can't keep this outbreak contained."

I understood. "Go home, Donna. No dishonor. You can make preparations and get everyone around you ready. No one doubts your ability. We all have that one thing that makes it different for us."

"What's your thing, John?" Donna asked, finally taking her tear-filled eyes off the kids.

"My family," I said, without hesitation. "If I thought they were in danger, I'd be doing what you are doing right now. Difference is, I have the guilt of not being there when I knew there was danger, and I lost my brother because of it."

Donna gathered up her pack. The sun was fully up, and was quickly burning off the fog of the river. Out in the parking lot, small forms were being revealed, remnants of the fight Charlie and I had.

Just before she left, Donna gave me a hug and kissed me on the cheek. "Give my love to Sarah and your boys. Keep them all safe, John."

"I will. Keep your kids safe, too." I returned the hug and watched as Donna walked over to one of the small cars. Duncan came over to watch her walk away.

"What a shame for us men," he said, shaking his head.

I knew what he meant. "People can't help what they are. I feel sorry for her, though."

Duncan looked at me. "Why?"

"There weren't that many lesbians before the Upheaval. I would imagine there are darned few afterwards."

"Good point."

I changed the subject. "We ready to roll?"

"Cycles are warming up, and we got a message from Tommy," Duncan said.

I brightened. That meant they were all still alive. "What is it?"

"'Hurry up here, or we're in deep shit.'"

Given how my day started, I took that as a really bad omen. I wondered if this was going to be our last stand, the last chance to keep what we had fought so long for. For a second, the rage flared, and I looked forward to the prospect of battle. When it settled, I realized I was as scared as I ever was.

"Let's go."

CHAPTER 42

"Talk to me!"

"I'm trying! Hang on. *Will you stop shooting for just one damn second?* Thank you! Take it outside! All right, where was I? Oh yeah, the zombies."

I cursed. Sometimes Tommy had a lousy way of relaying information, especially when he was in the middle of a zombie fight.

"All right. We hit the main horde further north than we had hoped for, but they were still travelling east. Luckily, several veteran groups had gotten the message and made a push south, forcing the zombies to re-route and head east closer to the river valley."

"How far north?"

"What?"

"Fuck it all. *How far north?*" I shouted into the transmitter. Duncan just shook his head while Charlie looked worried.

"Oh. We caught up with them near Oswego. A group of about twenty of us had made a stand just south of Aurora. We managed to push them south and took out about sixteen of them. They didn't try to fight; they just veered off, running east," Tommy said.

Charlie mouthed a few words at me, and I repeated them out loud to Tommy. "How many?" I knew it was a serious question, since the route of the zombies took them through some decently populated areas.

"As far as I could tell, we were looking at a horde of over three hundred."

Jesus. They must have run through some good-sized communities and somehow found some reinforcements. Still, it could be worse.

"Hey, John?"

"Yeah?"

"I heard a report that there are more coming up from Joslin. Apparently, there was a breach in the boundary. Not big enough for an adult zombie, but..." Tommy let that one hang and I just shook my head.

"How bad is that news?"

"Maybe five hundred, maybe more. It was second hand guessing from someone who said they saw them in the dark, but I don't doubt it."

I nearly dropped the transmitter. Anywhere from eight hundred to a thousand. I looked at Charlie and Duncan and they were as shocked as I was. I exhaled slowly before answering.

"All right. Where are you now?" I could still hear some firing in the background. It was sporadic, which told me the main fight was over.

"We're actually on the south end of Naperville, cleaning up the mess these kids left behind."

Charlie was a step ahead of me as he pulled a weathered map out and spread it on the dashboard. I looked at it quickly and made some calculations.

"All right. You need to get to I-55 and set up on the highway. You need to herd those kids to the river, and then head them south to the main bridge at 355. We'll get to the capital and round up everyone we can, and make defenses for that bridge. You have to keep them from going anywhere but that bridge, you understand. You have to!" I was getting louder and Duncan stopped me by shaking his head.

"I got you, John. Sarah sends her love by the way," Tommy said.

"I'll see all of you soon. The net tightens along the 55 corridor and the canal. No one gets past, and get them to the bridge," I repeated, already forming a strategy in my head. If it worked, we could finish this once and for all. If it failed, the world would finally surrender to the dead.

"Got it. By the way, we have about a hundred people here working this end. Tommy out."

That last was good news, and I needed it. I really hoped the capital would have what we need; otherwise, this was going to be a hard fight. I stepped out of the truck to address the assembled men and women.

"They've caught the main horde, but it's going to be tough. We'll need to get to the capital as fast as we can to set up defenses and make sure everyone is prepared. We don't have much time, so let's get moving." I kept it short; there wasn't any need to elaborate.

The sun rose steadily as we worked our way north. I rode in front, with Charlie and Duncan flanking me. I thought about Donna, and her decision to sit this one out. I felt guilty, because I might have been able to keep my brother alive had I sat this one out myself. Just as I thought it, I knew it was hopeless. I couldn't have sat out any more than I could send another person in my place to do something for me. It just wasn't in my nature.

Working our way around Joslin proved to be tougher than I had thought. There was a lot of debris and junk on the roads that I didn't remember being there before. Charlie gave me a look as we had to pass around another roadblock consisting of fallen trees, abandoned cars, and a strange collection of chairs and tables.

We crossed the river at Brandon Road, passing over the locks that haven't run in years. If we tried to open them now, they'd break apart and block the passage, which would accomplish exactly the opposite. We usually tried to avoid stupid when we could.

Patterson Road was a difficult trek, mostly because it was a route that people had taken hoping to avoid the congestion of the highways and main roads. Trouble was, everyone else had the same thought, and it was choked with cars as well. They were all rusty and had broken glass everywhere. No zombies were still sitting in the cars, but the debris slowed us down considerably. I figured it took us about an hour to go two miles.

CHAPTER 43

We finally reached Route 52, which took us north again. Charlie led the way this time, while I hung back and shouted a conversation with Duncan.

"*What's the plan?*"

"*We'll set up firing points, with fall back positions.*"

"*Just like Denver?*"

"*Just like Denver.*"

I was hoarse after a few minutes, so we rode in silence for a while. We rode under the I-80 junction, and had to be careful, since there were several cars all over the place. We had to get out and push one car around so we could pass by. A few were upside down, mostly because they had been thrown off the bridge. When we cleared the way, the guys on the crew looked forward to overpasses; since it wasn't often you had the chance to drop a car off a bridge.

Charlie took us east on Fourth avenue, which was strange since he had no more idea of where we were than I did. But I trusted his sense of direction, which found us north again and picking up Route 171. I gave Charlie a big thumbs up, and he replied by shrugging, since we both knew it was blind luck we weren't still cruising around Joslin.

We flew up Route 171, following the canal all the way up to Freeport. This was the road we needed to go to Leport. The sun was getting higher and I was getting more and more anxious, since I had the feeling we were running on borrowed time.

As we passed Freeport and made our way north, I saw several cars join our procession. I figured they were more veterans coming to join the fun, and I was glad to have them.

On the outskirts of town, we passed a small shop, just south of the 143rd street interchange. It was a gun shop, one of the three I visited many years ago, when the winds of the Upheaval were just starting to blow. A few memories played with my head, and I found it ironic I was back here after all this time. As we passed, I reminded myself that the last time I was here, Ellie was still alive. *So much since then. So much.* I thought to myself.

As we approached the on ramp, I signaled a stop. The cars and trucks spread out as they slowed, and turned the bike around so I could face everyone.

Thirty-six people looked at me, and I gave sober nods to the new people. They were indeed veterans, and I needed them as I had never needed them before.

"We're going to split here. Charlie, you take the group and get on the highway. Find your positions, and mark them. Stay tight. If they get here faster, you'll be the first ones they encounter. Charlie will fill you in on what you're facing. Use your cars and trucks, you know how. It's Denver all over again, Charlie," I said, winking at the big man. "Only we keep our clothes this time."

CHAPTER 44

Charlie gave me a slow grin, and rode down the on ramp, followed by the rest of the cars. Duncan and I turned around and rode hard for Leport, hoping like crazy we had enough time. I was also hoping there would be more veterans waiting for me.

We rode down the center of town, and there was a lot of activity. Everyone was working their way down to the riverbank, and when I hailed one person and asked why, I got a surprising answer.

"President Dot is ordering an evacuation. We're headed to the river. That's all I know." The man I spoke with was a young man, carrying two small children. His wife, a petite blonde was carrying what I presumed to be a stash of toys, food, and water. She also carried a rifle like she knew how to use it, and gave me a nod as she passed.

I couldn't figure out what Dot planned to do with all of the people down by the water, but she always had a plan, and I only knew her to be wrong a couple of times.

We threaded our way through the throngs, and I was getting impatient when Duncan decided to make a path by laying on his horn and yelling at the top of his lungs.

"*Make way! Talon coming through! Make way!*"

I made a mental note to smack him one for that later. Dozens of heads turned my way, and I raised a hand to several well-wishers. We had a job to do, and I needed to see Dot.

Down the main hill, we turned east by the church and rode to the house of the President. Dot was not there, but an assistant pointed us in the right direction.

We found Madame President at the piers, overseeing the loading of people onto several barges. The barges were waiting in a long line, and when one was filled, the towboat would push the line ahead and the next empty one would fill. Duncan and I watched with amazement. If we had utilized this method a long time ago, who knows how many people we might have saved?

Dot noticed us as we walked toward her. "John! Duncan! Thank God you're safe!" She hurried over and gave us each a hug.

"We just spoke with Tommy; they've stopped the horde and turned it this way. They took ten casualties, though."

I shook my head. These days, that was an unacceptable number. "Do they have enough people to push them to the main bridge? I have Charlie and about forty fighters setting up positions on 355."

Dot smiled and patted my arm. "Trust Tommy to handle his part. He did clear the route to Florida, remember?"

God, did I ever. If half the stuff I heard about that campaign was true, Tommy was a certifiable legend.

"All right, then. I need the front loader, four trailers, and a shitload of ammo." I outlined my plan quickly, knowing it would be an hour before we could get things in place. I was just grateful there was another ramp onto 355, which would bring us closer to the bridge and we wouldn't have to go far.

Dot turned to another aide. "John has priority on supplies, and command here." She turned back to me. "We'll hopefully be fully loaded in another thirty minutes. Where do you want me?"

I thought for a microsecond. "Get on the last barge, and make sure the people see you. Let them know what's going on, and let them know I ordered you aboard. I don't want them to be without a leader if all hell breaks loose."

Dot considered it, and then nodded. "We'll be on it." She looked to the bridge and the barges, then turned her wise eyes back to mine. "Guess you have to save us again, John."

I looked up to the bridge, exhaling slowly. "Yeah. One more time." I turned away and started to walk up the pier when Dot called out to me.

"John?"

"Yes?" I turned halfway back.

"I'm sorry about Iowa, and I'm so sorry about your brother."

I turned fully around and saw tears coming down the President's face. I nodded once.

"Thanks, Dot." I turned away and ran for my ride. I had a lot of preparing to do, and no damn time to do it in.

CHAPTER 45

I found Charlie setting up the last of the firing positions on the bridge. In the distance, I could see people sitting on top of their cars, lounging in the sun, and generally taking it easy. On the other side of the bridge, which was over a mile long, I could see activity as people moved around. I could sense their nervousness from here. They were going to be engaging the enemy, making themselves bait, and running for their lives. Duncan was with them, which made me feel better, but it was still rough.

Charlie came over when he saw me, although I was hard to miss. I was leading a convoy of four trucks and a front loader. The first two trucks had cargo carrier trailers, and the third was a pickup loaded with ammo and weapons. The fourth truck carried an improvised version of a fence, which consisted of knotted rope, four by fours, and a length of steel cable.

I got off my bike, and walked over to the truck with the fence. There were two men inside, and their faces were serious when I spoke to them.

"Set up the fence down by where the bridge is at least forty to fifty feet over the land. If they try to go around, I want them dead when they hit. Watch yourselves, and don't move until we signal you. If you go too early, we'll lose some for sure," I said.

The two men nodded and drove off. They were going to lay out a fence that was five feet high, made of wood and rope. The wood served as fence posts and the rope was the mesh that kept things in or out. Steel cable served as the support on the top and bottom. Essentially, we lay the fence flat, running the cable through the steel on top of the edges of the highway. The cable was attached to the truck tow bar, and when the truck pulled away, the fence came up and stayed there. It wouldn't work with hundreds of full size zombies in an open area, but it served us well here.

I motioned the two other trucks to go forward. Charlie stepped up and directed them to the left and right of the positions he had set up. The front loader followed, and was used to push the cargo containers into two places on the highway. The left one, about a hundred yards in front of where the fence was going to go, would turn the zombies into a killing zone on the right. The next container went one hundred yards in front of that on the opposite side, creating a second killing zone. As soon as the containers were in place, the people nearby climbed on top, sighting in their rifles and collecting ammo from the ammo truck.

When the front loader returned to our position, Charlie and I guided it in carefully turning the cars on their sides, creating another choke point should the zombies get this far. Hopefully, the firing from the containers would be enough, but you never knew.

"How you feeling, John?" Charlie asked, loading magazines for the AR-15 he had borrowed.

"About as good as can be expected, I guess," I said, loading up magazines as well.

"Think we have them this time?" Charlie asked.

I understood his concern. We had tried several times to bottle these little zombies up, but they always managed to elude us, either by slipping into the scenery or taking a route we hadn't thought of.

"The only thing that might be a problem is Tommy can't contain them and they slip away again. Hopefully, they're taking some serious losses and by the time the zombies hit us they'll be a lot fewer of them," I cautioned.

"Amen to that. I've had my fill of these things," Charlie said, putting in a loaded mag into his rifle and chambering a round. Flicking the safety on, he put it down and filled another magazine. "I never thought I'd say this…"

"What?"

"I actually miss fighting the slow, dumb ones. They seem almost tame to these little fuckers."

I laughed. "So do I man, so do I."

CHAPTER 46

Our laughter was cut short as a burst of firing drew our attention from the surrounding hills. It sounded like it was coming from the north of us, but with the echoes of the river valley it was hard to determine.

Charlie and I stood watching the hills, and there seemed to be some activity in the woods between the bridge we were on and the one further east. Charlie looked at me and I nodded. There was supposed to be people there, so that wasn't too much of a concern. There was more firing and it seemed very intense, more so than it should be.

I hefted my rifle and wished I had a scope in it. I couldn't see anything, and the nearest truck was the ammo truck that may or may not have held a radio. I looked down towards the river and saw that there were still people loading on the barges. If things broke through here, it was going to be a slaughter.

Suddenly, there was movement at the far end of the bridge. The truck Duncan was in, distributing ammunition was racing back towards us.

"I'm guessing this is not good news," Charlie said, stepping over to his motorcycle and starting it.

I followed suit, starting my cycle and watching the procession of cars rush towards me. I had a sinking feeling in my gut and knew it was about to get worse.

The truck screeched to a halt twenty feet from us, and the front doors flew open.

"John! Thank God! We have to move from here! Now!" Duncan yelled, leaning out the window while looking out over the river.

"What's the matter? If they're behind you, we're right where we need to be," I said, perplexed at this odd turn of events.

"Why did you pull our people off the line?" Charlie asked as the groups we set up ran towards us.

"Listen!" Duncan opened the door so we could hear the speakers from the radio.

The voice that came through was yelling information, and it was clear they were on the verge of panic.

"They've turned at the wrong place! Someone has to tell Talon they've turned at the wrong place! They're headed for the Leport Road bridge! Is anyone reading this? They're headed right for the barges if we don't stop them!"

I looked at Charlie and Duncan. This was the worst thing that could happen. We were in the wrong place. Our resources were a half mile away across a river valley, and useless here.

"Oh, Christ," I said, as another round of firing echoed off the hills.

Another voice cut in, calmer and in charge. "Get out, now. Half your people go to the river to protect the barges. Jump in if you get charged. The other half, get to the other bridge and hold it for as long as you can. Do *not* let them flank us. We'll draw them away from the line, kill as many as you can."

I recognized Tommy's voice and not for the first time, was I glad to hear it.

"We need to get over there as fast as we can. They're running out of time, and they need us now," I said.

Charlie pointed across the river. "We're out of time, too."

We could just make out a group of people running like their lives depended on it onto the bridge. They stopped, fired at something we couldn't see, then ran forward again. It was methodical, well executed, and suicidal.

"Goddamn," I said. "And we tipped over the extra vehicles."

"Come on, let's get this one back." Charlie threw himself against the car, moving it slightly. I followed suit, with Duncan next to me and on the next rush; we knocked the car back over.

"They can use that one," I said, waving my arms over my head. I pointed at the car and then pointed at the other bridge. The lead runner waved me on, and I turned back to Charlie.

"We going?" he asked.

"Just now. Follow me," I said. I didn't pay any attention to speed limits or road conditions. I just rode like a bat out of hell, with Charlie and Duncan right on my wheels.

CHAPTER 47

I flew up the exit to 127th street, and then raced towards Leport Road. I nearly slid as I turned hard and I gunned the engine, gritting my teeth in frustration as the bike refused to grow wings and fly. I could hear Charlie's bike screaming behind me, and the roar of the truck as Duncan tried to keep up.

I rocketed down the hill towards the river, and nearly dumped the bike as I approached the small crowds of people waiting to get on the barges. Dot was there, and she looked at me in worry as I braked hard.

"Get on the barges! Get the hell out of here! The zombies are on the bridge, they're headed right for you!" I pointed at a man standing by Dot. "You! Get the people with weapons ready! They might need them now! Go! Go!" I didn't wait to say any more, I just kicked the bike into gear and yanked on the throttle. I nearly unseated myself in my haste to get moving. I waved Duncan to go up the left side of the bridge, since we'd need him there.

As I ran the bike up the tall bridge, I could hear more firing. It seemed to be coming from right in front of me, and as I reached the top, I could see the group still running, still pausing to throw lead behind them, and then running again. On the far side of the bridge, a massive horde advanced steadily. They left behind their dead, a trail of little zombie breadcrumbs.

I brought the bike to a stop, turning it sideways and backing it up to the wall. I put the kickstand down and watched as Charlie did the same. The two bikes blocked most of the road, and on the other side, Duncan turned the truck as well. It covered the two lanes decently, but a big rush would blow by, nearly undelayed. It couldn't be helped.

We could see the group running towards us, and there was a long stretch of level ground that would have been useful as a firing lane, but we couldn't shoot for fear of hitting our comrades. Behind them, an undulating wall of zombies ran, and even from this distance, we could hear their wheezing cries and clacking teeth. If any of that group fell, they'd be dead.

In one motion, the group stopped, and paused to throw bullets at their pursuers. I could hear the sharp crack of rifles and the lower pitch of heavier caliber guns, and my heart suddenly leapt to my throat.

"Oh, my God. That's Sarah's gun," I said to myself, raising my carbine. Charlie heard me, and his gun whipped up as well.

Duncan saw the two of us, and looked carefully at the runners. "That's Tommy, Sarah and Rebecca. Dammit, what do we do?"

I held the rifle steady, and put full faith in their ability to move, and in what I had to do. "We hold the line," I said without emotion.

Out of the corner of my eye, I saw Charlie stare at me for a long time, and then slowly nod his head. We were the only ones standing between those zombies and the people exposed on those barges, and if we lost it here, then everything was lost. There wouldn't be anyone to stand in the way of the zombies, and they'd wipe out everything we had built for the last seven years.

I went to the far side of the road, noticing that the group stayed pretty close to the center of the bridge. Charlie jumped the median and set up a firing position on the far side. Duncan stood up on the median and signaled the group by firing once in the air and waving his arms. The men and women responded by running harder, but it was easy to see they were at the end of their steam. The Leport Bridge was over a mile long, and it wasn't easy to run that entire distance at full speed.I laid out my magazines on the barrier next to me. I had six in all, and fully loaded that gave me nearly two hundred shots. I had three magazines for my 1911, although I doubted I was going to use that gun much at all. I stepped a little forward and put my trench hawk and pickaxe on the barrier. Saving even the half second it would take to draw them from their sheaths.

Charlie saw what I was doing and did the same thing, placing his 'hawks on the wall, and putting his magazines within easy reach. Duncan stayed on the median, yelling out encouragement as he aimed his rifle.

Charlie suddenly fired, and I could see a zombie stumble and fall, only to get up again. Charlie cursed, and I didn't bother with any smack talk for his accuracy. He was shooting at a softball sized target well over three hundred yards away with open sight. If he'd hit, I'd have been stunned.

Duncan wasn't so kind. "Throw a rock next time, doof."

Charlie growled but he smiled, too. He knew Duncan was trying to loosen the tension, but *his* wife wasn't running for her life in front of a horde of vicious zombies.

The group stopped to fire again, and they were only about two hundred yards away. I could see them much more clearly, and was glad to see Tommy, Sarah, and Rebecca still alive. I almost took a shot at the pursuing zombies, but knew I had to wait a little longer. I wanted to kill them, but at this range, it would have been more luck than skill.

A sound behind got my attention and I turned to see two cars racing towards me. One was the car we had turned over on the other bridge, and a second was unknown to me. But they both held more people and weapons, and they were able to block the roads better with more cars. Charlie sent one man and the second car careening down the road to get to the other side to help block that side.

I didn't waste time. "Spread out, ten on a side. Don't fire until our people are clear. Save your ammo, we're going to need every round."

No one spoke; they just did as they were told. A lane was left clear for our people, and they were a hundred yards away, now. I could do nothing for them, so I just waited with my rifle up and my sights on the oncoming horde. The river stretched out on either side of me, sparkling in the sun. The valley contained multitudes of colored trees, brilliant in the sunlight of the day. I'd seen the same thing from Starved Rock hundreds of times, but there was something special about this place. It was where I had decided to start over, where we made a safe place to live and take back what we had lost in the Upheaval. For hundreds of people it was home. If anyone asked why I fought, that would be my answer. So we could have a home.

"Here they come!" Duncan shouted from his slight perch.

CHAPTER 48

Men and women sighted their rifles over hoods, trunks, truck beds and motorcycles. We needed to make the first few volleys devastating, or all would be lost.

Tommy, Sarah, Rebecca, and about ten other people came running forward, quickly climbing over our barricade. Sarah slumped into my arms, breathing heavily.

"Thank…God…you're…safe…" She panted.

"Back at you." I guided and carried her over to the other people who were leaning back or leaning over, gulping air.

"I'm glad you're all safe. We have some work to do, and I need you all to be the back up point. If we retreat, wait for us to clear, and then fire," I said, helping Sarah to lean against a median.

I kissed her on the top over her head. "Gotta go to work, babe, I'm happy you're here." I pointed to the truck blocking the road. "Ammo's over there, load up."

She looked up at me. "No where else," Sarah said firmly. She stood and started over to the truck, waving a couple others to help.

I went back to the line. Tommy was waiting for me.

"We're good on this end. But it was close." He didn't say anything more, and I wondered how close it really was.

"Wish we could block the other end," I said as the first of the zombies came into view. They had stopped running, and were jogging slightly, their little feet slapping the pavement nearly in unison.

Tommy smiled. "Got that covered at least, thank you very much."

"How?" They were out there on their own as far as I could tell.

"You'll see. Here they come." Tommy shifted his rifle and stood over one of the motorcycles.

I went over to the side where my magazines were. As I picked up one and held it in my left hand, I noticed a small bird looking at me from about fifteen feet away. It was a sparrow, and by the look of it, it was pretty well fed. It cocked its head at me, and for no reason I could think of, I winked at it. To my surprise, the bird peeped once at me, looked down the road, and flew off, circling under the bridge. I watched it until it was out of sight, then looked at the oncoming horde, which was now only twenty yards away and closing quickly. There was nothing left to do.

"*Cut them down!*" I yelled, as I aimed quickly and fired. Several rifles fired at once, and the entire front row of the zombies on both sides of the road flew back, spraying their brains and black blood over their comrades to the rear. The rest of the zombies clacked their teeth and charged as one.

I emptied my first magazine, and quickly reloaded the rifle with a new one. I kept firing, and saw that the others were firing as well. We were blasting holes in their lines, but they still kept coming. Every one I put down for good would be replaced with another. Some were knocked off their feet, only to get up again. Others were hit in the spine and dragged themselves across the road, scraping their dead flesh from their fingers as they clawed forward. Some were hit in the neck and went down paralyzed, only able to thrash their heads in futile rage.

We were able to hold them at bay with our firing, but I knew we were going to get into it as soon as we started to run out of ammo. There was no helping it; it was going to get ugly.

Already I could see parts of the zombie line able to advance as someone took a second or two longer to reload. All it took was a few seconds, and they gained yards on us. There didn't seem to be any end to the zombies, and I was running down to my last magazine.

Charlie started it.

"I'm out!" He yelled. He set his rifle down and picked up his tomahawks. In a rare display of emotion, he stood on the median, slammed the heads of his weapons together in a huge metallic clang, and roared his defiance at the zombies. Anyone unfamiliar with Charlie would have thought a Viking berserker had suddenly appeared on the scene.

I kept firing until I heard two more people yell they were out as well. "Fall back!" I yelled over the shooting. "Secondary line! Fall back, now!"

The groups on both sides of the road retreated slowly, still firing as they went back. The second line was only twenty feet away, but it felt like a hundred as the horde advanced towards our makeshift barricades. I picked up my pick and trench hawk, and fired my last rounds as I walked slowly backwards to the line.

As soon as I crossed, Tommy called out.

"Pick your targets! Stay on your side. Don't cross the center unless you have to!" The rifles started firing, but not as rapidly as before. They were shooting around the motorcycles and the trucks, and I watched ruefully as a bullet tore through the seat of one of the BMW's. I cheered up when I realized it was Duncan's.

Sarah and Rebecca were side-by-side, firing in turns. Bodies piled up around the edges and began to make another barricade. When the corpses reached about two feet high, the horde stopped advancing and it seemed like they were going to run the other way.

"Tommy...?" I asked in the lull.

"Wait for it. They were told to hide until the last of the zombies passed them," he said cryptically.

I fired my last shot at a zombie five year old crawling across the hood of the truck. His body slumped down, and then slid off, leaving a dark trail across the metal.

"Tommy, I'm really not in the mood," I said, placing my rifle against the median wall.

"Here they come."

CHAPTER 49

I heard them before I saw them. Metal was scraping on asphalt, grinding and pushing. It was a harsh, nasty sound, nearly as bad as scratching fingernails across a chalkboard. I looked around and everyone was wincing in some fashion.

On the hill, six snowplows, three on each side of the road, came slowly over the crest. They were spaced in such a way that the blades overlapped, and left no room whatsoever for a zombie to slip past. If they tried, they'd get crushed between the blade and the wall, or they would get pushed over the edge and fall to the river sixty feet below.

When they reached about two hundred yards from us, they stopped, and the people in the cabs got out and started firing down on the Z's. In the crisp fall air, with the leaves changing color, and the sun glancing off the shiny steel blades of the plow, it was a beautiful sight.

"Well done, Tommy. Well done," I said in admiration. It was a brilliant strategy. The Z's had nowhere to go but straight at us, and we were keeping them bottled up. If we could get some reinforcements in the next ten minutes, we'd be good to finish these guys off.

"Thanks," I thought… "Oh, shit." Tommy looked at the barricade and whipped up his rifle, firing methodically.

I looked and my heart sank. The plows had given the zombies a reason to rush, and they came barreling at our barricades, pushing aside dead comrades and climbing over the only thing left separating them from us.

"Watch yourselves!" I shouted. "Pair up! Watch your backs!" I ran over to the other side of the road. "Charlie! On me!" I turned back to Sarah and Rebecca, who were paired up already. Sarah held what looked like two short swords. I had no idea where she got them, but I prayed she was good with them. Rebecca had what looked like a baseball bat with short fingers of metal protruding from the end. Whatever the hell it was, it sure looked effective.

"Sarah, you and Rebecca are the end of the line. If it gets past us, it can't get past you," I said, taking a position in the front with

Charlie. Duncan and Tommy were on the other side, slightly further apart, since Duncan was hefting his long sword.

"You got it, babe. Hey, John?"

"What?"

"If we survive this, I'm going to screw your brains out."

I looked back at Sarah and she gave me a lascivious wink while licking her lips. It was so absurd I just chuckled. I glanced at Charlie and he was about to say something when Rebecca chimed in.

"Goes double for you, big boy."

Charlie turned red and as I laughed and I could feel the cold fire of battle building within. I had chased these bastards across two states. They had killed my friends and killed my brother. My breathing started to slow and my hands gripped my weapons tighter. I inhaled and growled at the same time when the first little zombie came at me.

"Die, you fucker!" I snarled, crushing its skull with my pick. I kicked the body out of the way and waited for the next one. Tommy and Duncan were busy on the east side while Charlie and I waited on more to clear the obstacles.

"John?"

"Yes, Charlie?"

"How come we keep getting into shit like this?"

"Because we're a couple of morons who haven't got sense enough to stay home and not answer the damn phone."

"That would explain it. Thanks."

"You're welcome. On your left."

Charlie began killing with his tomahawks, using both hands to devastate the zombies. Kids flew back with their heads cracked, or the slumped down with severed necks. Black zombie fluid flew in great arcs as Charlie fought and killed.

I had little time to admire his handiwork. I sidestepped a lunge and backhanded a kid on the back of his neck, throwing him behind me where Sarah finished him off with a quick stab to the head. I thrust the pick forward into the teeth of another, dragging it forward to be spiked with my 'hawk. I reversed the spike and slammed the blade end into another who was trying to get in between Charlie and myself.

I got down on one knee and put my axe on the ground. I swung my pickaxe with both hands, snapping backs and cracking skulls as the zombie kids came at me in wave after wave after wave. Several got past me, and got past Tommy and Duncan, only to be finished by Rebecca and Sarah. Zombie bits surrounded Duncan, and Tommy looked strangely uncomfortable to be covered in little Z parts.

I killed until there was a ring of dead around me; Charlie had a similar ring, only his was deeper since he tended to fling their corpses further than I did. But they kept coming. They were swinging at me with both hands, trying to get hold of me somewhere, anywhere, so I couldn't fight them off and they could overwhelm me. All they needed was a second of hesitation and it was over.

I couldn't give it to them. I swung, killed, knocked over, killed, kicked, killed, and piled up my pay to the ferryman. On a back swing, I missed the head of the boy I was aiming at and buried the blade in his neck. He grasped the axe and pulled, yanking it out of my grasp. I swung hard at another zombie, and then pulled my long bladed knife out of its sheath. I didn't have time to switch to a more effective grip, I just speared the grinning zombie in the eye, taking him down to the ground. I pulled the blade out as I slammed the pick on another head, sheathing it quickly. I yanked out my tomahawk with a wet squelch.

"Mine," I said to the corpse. "No touching."

I lost track of how many I killed, and when a lull occurred, I actually went to one knee, I was that tired. Bodies were piled around me and I had little room to maneuver. I stood up and saw Charlie finish off the last one on his side, and on my right Tommy and Duncan were wiping off weapons.

Charlie rolled his shoulders and flexed his hands. "That it?" He asked, addressing no one in particular.

I waited. On the other side of the median, they had fared better than we did. More of the zombies had been on our side, and they actually were stepping forward, looking to clear their lane.

CHAPTER 50

I signaled to the crew to follow me, holding a hand up to Sarah and the rest. The four of us carefully made our way around the barricade, walking carefully along the barrier which separated the two lanes. On the other side was simply slaughter. Corpses filled the road from one side to the other, and here and there was slight movement from zombies that weren't quite dead but couldn't move to attack us. We stayed along the median and the far barricade, quietly working our way through the destruction.

I had to admit, I was sad to see so much of the future wasted. So many precious children taken away from life before they knew what it really was. They didn't ask to be turned, didn't ask to be ripped from their parents, didn't ask to be killed on a road far from home. They would never even be buried near people who could mourn them, and remember them from the little life they did have.

"Did we get the leader?" Duncan asked, poking a moving Z in the head with his sword.

"Couldn't tell you," I said. "I never got a clear look at her, so if she's here, she's dead."

"No, she's not," Charlie said, pointing with his tomahawk.

Over by the plows, a single zombie was cowering under the curve of the blade. The people on the plows had their rifles trained on the spot, but from their vantage point, they didn't have a shot.

When we were within fifty yards, she became aware of us. She glared hate and frustration as she swung her hands at us. Even at that distance, I could hear her frenzied wheezing.

I guess I never thought I would be here, facing an enemy I had chased across two states, losing several good people and a brother in the process. I was filled with hate and rage, and I threw my weapons down as I advanced on her.

My companions called out to me as I moved forward, yelling at me to stop. I advanced to within twenty yards and I could see her much more clearly. She was light grey, with black eyes. The white of her eyes were black as well, and it was an eerie thing to see. Her hair was short and greasy, missing in several places. She bared her teeth at me, and I could see they were chipped and jagged, black from clotted blood.

I stopped at fifteen yards and she hissed, looking up and around. If I didn't know better, I would have figured she would have tried to run.

Like hell. I pulled my Springfield and fired every round at her, beating her into the plow, and shredding her with hollow points. I didn't even aim all that well, I just shot the magazine dry, then replaced it. I waited to see if she would fall, and when she didn't, I fired six more times. One bullet managed to hit her spine and dropped her to the ground. She clawed her way forward, dragging herself slowly in my direction. I walked up to meet her, and when I was about six feet away, I knelt down and waited. She crawled within three feet and stretched a hand towards me as she looked up at my face. She didn't look much better close up, I had to admit.

I quickly brought the .45 up and fired. The heavy bullet rocked her head back as it blew out the back of her skull, sending bits of dark brain matter all over the road. She slumped down and was still.

I holstered my gun, and looked down at the hand that had stretched towards me. On the wrist was a small bracelet, and there were little white beads on it. There seemed to be some letters, so I turned the wrist over and saw "Ellen" written in flowers on the beads.

I stood up as it all came flooding back in a rush, the first few weeks of the Upheaval, the fight to survive, and the little girl I had rescued from that scum at the pharmacy. I never knew what happened to her after she left with Todd and his family, but somewhere she must have left them, grew up some, and gotten infected.

"Holy shit." I said aloud. I had nothing else to say.

Charlie, Duncan and Tommy came walking up, likely wanting to see what had caused so much trouble for so many people.

"That it?" Charlie asked.

"I think so," I said. "There may be some cleanup to do around the edges, but that should be it."

"What a mess," Duncan said, kneeling down by the corpse. "Wonder what was different about her that caused the virus to change so much?"

"Don't know, don't care," Tommy said, shaking off some zombie goo from his weapon.

"I guess I just don't understand why there was this need to go east. Why that way?" Duncan persisted.

Charlie shrugged, but I threw out an answer.

"Probably the strongest urge we have as humans, and even in death it won't escape us." I postulated.

"What urge?" Duncan asked.

"The desire to go home," I said.

CHAPTER 51

We left the clean up to the people of Leport, which at first seems like a rotten thing to do, but since there were already six plows ready to go right at the battle scene, if it took longer than an hour, I'd be surprised.

As we made our way back to the other groups, Charlie pulled me aside.

"I have to tell you something," he said.

This was different. "All right, what is it?" I asked, curious.

"Every time we fought, I always had something in my mind that I was fighting for, be it Julia, Rebecca, or you guys. Something that made me hit a little harder, fight a little longer, just something," Charlie confided.

"I can relate. Same goes for me. For a long time it was Jake, then Sarah, then the rest of you combined." I understood this part pretty well.

"This time it was different," Charlie said.

"How so?"

Charlie looked up the road to where Sarah and Rebecca were waiting. "All I could think about was getting laid if I survived."

I tried not to grin too broadly as I clapped Charlie on the shoulder. "Me, too," I said. "Me, too."

We gathered up the rest of our crew after an appropriate reuniting, and spent the next hour cleaning our weapons and watching the town of Leport disgorge from the barges. They never did get everyone loaded, and it would have been a bad thing if we had failed to stop the zombies on the bridge.

We met with the veterans who had answered the call, and I gave each of them a personal thanks. If they hadn't fought as well as they had, who knows where this fight would have ended.

As we walked up the street, I met with Dot and gave her the news. She didn't seem all that surprised that the little zombie leader was just trying to go back to home. But then, nothing seemed to surprise Dot, so I just let it go.

While leaving her house, a black cat came scampering around the corner of the porch. It was an older cat, and looked like it had seen its share of hard times. It looked at me with half closed eyes, as if it was trying to remember to tell me something.

The cat looked familiar, and I pointed it out to Dot.

"Where'd you get the cat?"

Dot smiled. "He just showed up one day, rolling in like he owned the place. He made himself at home, and we've gotten used to him. He's a bit funny. He likes to sleep in cabinets, so you get surprised once in a while."

That jogged a memory loose. I called Tommy over.

"Tommy, does that cat look familiar?"

Tommy looked, and then did a double take. "Hang on." He walked over to the cat, and after letting it smell his hand and approve of him, Tommy picked up the cat and held it carefully in the crook of his arm. He looked hard between the ears of the cat and set him down gently. Tommy looked at me and nodded.

"I'll be damned. Well, good to see you, Zeus." I left the contented cat to stay with Dot; he didn't belong to us any more than he belonged to anyone. If a cat that had managed to survive a fifteen hundred mile journey wanted to set up shop in the president's house, who was I to stop him?

52

We rode home the next morning, and Sarah had made good on her promise the night before. Duncan complained about the seat on his cycle, but nothing else went awry.

About noon, we pulled into our home, and I spent the next several hours just holding my children and listening to my father talk about his travels and what he was teaching the boys. I gave my dad a look when I asked Jake to get something for me and he answered with a 'Hoo-ah!' We'd be talking about that later.

Later that evening, Sarah joined me on the porch as I watched the river roll past. Charlie and Rebecca were sitting at the table nearby, and we all just took in the fall air.

I told them about the little girl and what I thought had happened to her, and why she seemed intent on heading east. They were incredulous, but they didn't doubt me. With everything we had seen, nothing was completely impossible.

As night fell, and we all worked our way to the bedrooms, I stopped to kiss my kids goodnight. Sarah was waiting for me in the hallway.

"Do you think this is it?" She asked, slipping her arms around my waist.

"What is?"

"Have we seen the last of the hordes?" She looked up into my eyes, and even though it was dark, I could still see her looking intently at me.

"I wish I could say. Every time I think we can just live, something else comes along. I pray to God we're done. All I want to do is get busy living, raising my sons, and growing old with you." I kissed her gently.

"But who knows? Somewhere down the line, another crisis may rear its zombified head," I said. "I just hope its twenty years down the road."

"Why?" Sarah asked as she guided me to the bedroom.

"So the kids can deal with it. We saved their butts, they can save ours."

Sarah just laughed as she shut the door.

I lay down on my side of the bed and just stared at the ceiling for a while. I ached in body and heart, and it would be a long time before both healed completely. But I thought about my kids, and figured in the end, it would all work out.

I looked at my .45 as it rested in its accustomed place on top of my nightstand. In a rare fit of optimism, I put it in the drawer and slowly closed it.

THE END

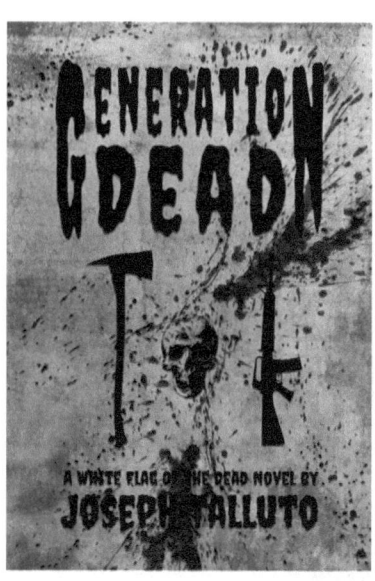

Jake Talon and his brother Aaron grew up in the zombie apocalypse. All they have ever known is a world constantly threatened with extinction from the undead hordes which roamed the land. Taught by their father to survive and live, the two men drift, unsure of their future. As Jake and Aaron try to figure out what they were meant to do with this world of theirs, someone has plans to bring the zombies back.

Generation Dead marks the beginning of an exciting new stand alone series from Joseph Talluto and takes place some 20 years after the conclusion of The White Flag of the Dead series.

Mankind is on the brink of extinction. A deadly plague sweeps the globe like a tsunami causing the dead to rise and prey on the living. When there's no more room in Hell is a horror/action story set in a post-apocalyptic world filled with suspense, drama, humour, grief and action.

While one brother fights his way home through the horrors and confusion of a savage landscape from the 'Meat Grinder' that is Iraq, the other finds himself as the leader of a rag-tag band of survivors striving to survive against the onslaught of the dead.

www.severedpress.com

Dr. Jebediah Stone never believed in zombies until he had to shoot one. Now they're mutating into a new species, capable of reproducing, and the only defence is 'Blue Juice', a vaccine distilled from the blood of rare individuals immune to the zombie plague. Dr. Stone's missing wife is one of these unwilling 'munies', snatched by the military under the Judgment Day Protocol.It's a new, dangerous world filled with zombies, street gangs, and merciless Hunters desperate for a shot of blue juice. Has the world turned on mankind? Is Mortuus Venator the new ruler of earth?

www.severedpress.com

ICE STATION ZOMBIE
JE GURLEY

For most of the long, cold winter, Antarctica is a frozen wasteland. Now, the ice is melting and the zombies are thawing. Arctic explorers Val Marino and Elliot Anson race against time and death to reach Australia, but the Demise has preceded them and zombies stalk the streets of Adelaide and Coober Pedy.

www.severedpress.com

The Coalition

When the dead rose to destroy the living, Ron Cutter learned to survive. While so many others died, he thrived. His life is a constant battle against the living dead. As he casts his own bullets and packs his shotgun shells, his humanity slowly melts away.

Then he encounters a lost boy and a woman searching for a place of refuge. Can they help him recover the emotions he set aside to live? And if he does recover them, will those feelings be an asset in his struggles, or a danger to him?

THE STATE OF EXTINCTION: the first installment in the **COALITON OF THE LIVING** trilogy of Mankind's battle against the plague of the Living Dead. As recounted by author **Robert Mathis Kurtz.**

www.severedpress.com

RANCID

Nothing ever happens in the middle of nowhere or in Virginia for that matter. This is why Noel and her friends found themselves on cloud nine when one of their favorite hardcore bands happened to be playing a show in their small hometown. Between the meteor shower and the short trip to the cemetery outside of town after the show, this crazy group of friends instantly plummet from those clouds into a frenzied nightmare of putrefied horror.

Is this sudden nightmare related to the showering meteors or does this small town hold even darker secrets than the rotting corpses that are surfacing?

"Zombies in small town America, a corporate conspiracy, fast paced action and a satisfying body count- what's not to like? Just don't get too attached to any character; they may die or turn zombie soon enough!" - Mainak Dhar, bestselling author of Alice in Deadland and Zombiestan

www.severedpress.com

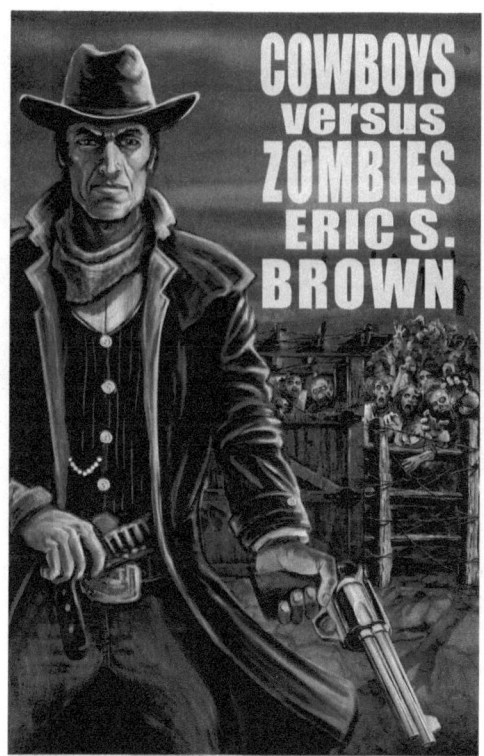

COWBOYS VS ZOMBIES

Dilouie is a killer. He's always made his way in life by the speed of his gun hand and the coldness of his remorseless heart. Life never meant much to him until the world fell apart and they awoke. Overnight, the dead stopped being dead. Hungry corpses rose from blood splattered streets and graves. Their numbers were unimaginable and their need for the flesh of the living insatiable.

The United States is no more. Washed away in a tide of gnashing teeth and rotting, clawing hands. Dilouie no longer kills for money and pleasure but to simply keep breathing and to see the sunrise of the next dawn. . . And he is beginning to wonder if even men like him can survive in a world that now belongs to the dead?

TIMOTHY
MARK TOFO

Timothy was not a good man in life and being
undead did little to improve his disposition.
Find out what a man trapped in his own mind
will do to survive when he wakes up to find
himself a zombie controlled by a self-aware
virus.

www.severedpress.com